A HUNDRED THOUSAND REASONS FOR REVENGE

Against a backdrop of Hollywood glamour, greed, betrayal and bizarre cults, a man is found dead in circumstances that defy explanation. Is it murder? An accident? Suicide? Or something else? FBI Special Agent Brett Dawson and unorthodox private investigator Vincent Stoker join forces to discover the truth. Following the grisly and perplexing leads from an unlikely start in small-town America through the mansions and dives of Los Angeles, their path takes them to a final showdown in the desert where they must put their faith in the unbelievable to survive.

EDMUND GLASBY

A HUNDRED THOUSAND REASONS FOR REVENGE

Complete and Unabridged

LINFORD
Leicester

First published in Great Britain

First Linford Edition
published 2019

*A catalogue record for this book is available
from the British Library.*

ISBN 978–1–4448–4170–1

Published by
F. A. Thorpe (Publishing)
Anstey, Leicestershire

Set by Words & Graphics Ltd.
Anstey, Leicestershire
Printed and bound in Great Britain by
T. J. International Ltd., Padstow, Cornwall

This book is printed on acid-free paper

1

Dead Men Tell No Tales

Special Agent Brett Dawson had watched with some measure of morbid curiosity as the bullet-riddled corpse of Jack Dupont, a notorious gangland criminal with Mafia connections, had been extricated from a black body bag then meticulously stripped and carefully laid out on the autopsy table. He was not by nature particularly squeamish, his senses bolstered by the fact that over the course of his fifteen years in the San Francisco-based unit of the FBI he had seen far more dead bodies than the average person.

Dupont had been on the Bureau's most wanted list for several years and a team of operatives had been carefully piecing together enough evidence to put him away for the rest of his life.

Recently, Dawson had finally persuaded the hardened criminal to turn state's evidence in the hope of convicting three of the worst Mafia bosses in California. Looking at the ruined body on the table, he silently cursed the fact that someone else must have been very aware of what was going on and had ordered the hit.

'Say, Dawson. Are you still working on that Steinzegger case?' asked Herbert Grant, the medical examiner, as he shone a pencil torch into the cadaver's eyes and examined them.

'No. That was wrapped up back in April,' Dawson replied.

'How did it go?'

'It was weird. Very weird. Still, we got it all sorted out in the end.'

'I've heard it had something to do with the Kennedy assassination. Is that right?'

Dawson smiled. 'Oh, come on, Grant. You think everything's related to that.'

Grant looked up. 'But you're not actually denying it, are you? Thirteen years it's been and I've still not heard a satisfactory explanation.' He picked up a small camera and took several photographs of the corpse. 'Don't play the ignorant with me. You must know

2

something about it. You've got access to all those confidential files that — '

'Why don't you quit interrogating me and concentrate on Mr Dupont?' Dawson interrupted. 'I only know what you know.' It was true. He had never been told any more than the general public but privately he thought the whole thing stank of a high-level cover-up. There were rumours and countless conspiracy theories circling but nothing tangible. Past experience had taught him that it was usually better to keep his suspicions to himself.

'Yeah, sure. I'll find out one day. Mark my words, the truth will come out.' Having now obtained his photographic evidence, Grant set down the camera. 'This guy will be pretty routine. The kind I've done a hundred times over.'

'Then I'll expect the report on my desk in an hour,' Dawson joked.

'Well, you know the basics anyway — death by multiple gunshot wounds. Standard nine millimetre parabellum rounds. Fired at close range. There's also a contusion just above his right eye but I suspect that's where he fell, rather than an intentional injury. Where was he found?'

'Law enforcement officers were alerted to a shooting in Potrero Hill. The victim was discovered just behind an Irish bar called *O'Malley's*.'

'*O'Malley's*? I've been there a couple of times,' Grant said. 'A rough joint, still they do a damn good whisky. Anyway, I suppose I'd better get started.' He reached for his microphone and signalled for Dawson to be quiet as he began to speak. 'Jack Dupont. Caucasian male — six feet two inches . . . '

Before leaving the mortuary, Dawson took one last look at the bloody, cold dead body of the mobster, wondering to himself just what information they had missed out on.

$\star$ $\star$ $\star$

The following morning, Dawson sat at his desk typing up the final details pertaining to Dupont's demise. It galled him that all the methodical and painstaking work he and his colleagues had done on the case was now practically worthless. They could have had a massive impact on organised crime in the state if Dupont had lived and become a witness for the prosecution. As it was, there was no hope of getting another informant of that calibre.

The Deputy Director was said to be furious and ready to apportion blame wherever he felt fit.

Whatever happened, it was not going to help any of their careers.

Doubtless, someone would be tasked with tracking down the killer and, more importantly, his employer, but as far as Dawson's involvement was concerned, the case was closed. He pulled the final piece of paper out of the typewriter and, content with what he had written, slipped it into the Dupont file and set it on the side of his desk. He rose to his feet, put his black jacket back on, straightened his tie, picked up the report and headed for what was likely to be an uncomfortable interview. As he turned into the corridor, he was surprised to see the tall, bald-headed figure of the Deputy Director himself, William McMasters, walking towards him.

'Dawson, good.'

'I have the Dupont report here, sir,' Dawson began.

'I'll read it later,' McMasters said dismissively. 'Right now you're needed in Huntersville. A call's come through from the local sheriff requesting our assistance and, as you're now suddenly available, you drew the short straw.'

'But — '

'Talk to Special Agent Dean. He'll give you all the details we have but it appears that Huntersville has got itself an unpleasant little murder. Might be nothing, but go and check it out.'

'Yes, sir. At once,' Dawson replied, wondering what was so important that McMasters had foregone the pleasure of hauling him over the coals. Turning on his heel, somewhat relieved, he went in search of Paul Dean who he finally found making himself a coffee in the staff canteen.

Dean glanced round as he heard Dawson approach. 'Brett. Off to Huntersville then? You're not going to believe this one.'

The coastal fog which had fallen over Huntersville — thirty miles south of San Francisco — and its immediate surroundings was gradually beginning to dissipate as Dawson turned his car off Benevolent Street and followed the directions he had been given to the local football ground. He had never been here before but the town's layout and its municipal buildings were all too familiar; reminiscent of so many of the small Californian semi-urban developments he had visited during the course of his career. At thirty-seven, he had seen and experienced more than many twice his age; his time spent working on a whole range of criminal cases, mostly homicides, hardening his outlook on life. He suspected that it was primarily due to his well-cultivated cynicism that he had been given his latest assignment and even he would have to admit that, from the brief Dean had given him, it had the potential of presenting some 'unique' challenges.

Taking a right at the intersection,

Dawson found himself heading into the outskirts of Huntersville and a few minutes later he saw the parked sheriff's car, its lights flashing, and pulled up alongside it. He checked his reflection in the rear-view mirror and smoothed his hair back before unbuckling his seatbelt and getting out of his vehicle. It was cold and damp and what sunlight there was struggled to filter through the clinging mist. Just at the edge of his vision, he could make out the tenebrous outline of another vehicle. Advancing towards it, he saw its crumpled hood and the tyre marks where it had obviously skidded off the road and hit a tree. It looked as though one of the rear tyres had imploded.

A young, fresh-faced deputy, pen and pad in hand, was peering intently into the back seat. He straightened as the Special Agent approached.

'FBI.' Dawson briefly flashed his badge. 'I'm looking for Sheriff Baker-man.'

'He's over there,' the deputy said, pointing. 'In the field. That's where the body is . . . relatively speaking, I suppose.'

Dawson nodded, his interest piqued by the somewhat cryptic response. The details he had been given of the death had been sketchy and frankly hard to believe. Yet, in some way, this was to be expected for it took something out of the ordinary to necessitate the Bureau's involvement. The Huntersville sheriff had clearly felt out of his depth and, unusually, was eager for help with a death that defied explanation.

'I'll take you over, if you like,' the deputy offered.

'After you, then,' Dawson said. The mist was thick enough to shroud the playing field and it took a minute or two before he could discern the familiar, bident-shaped goalpost. Despite his training, he felt a sick anticipation at what he was about to see. Sure enough, once he drew close, his stomach turned over.

The blood-soaked corpse of a be-suited man lay slumped face down over the crossbar at one corner of the goalpost; back arched, arms and legs dangling. For two thirds of its length, the right-hand, normally white, thirty foot high upright was smeared with blood and an obscene trail of viscera.

A stocky man, who was clearly the sheriff, stood gazing up at the corpse.

'Sheriff Bakerman?' asked Dawson, unable to take his eyes off the gruesome sight. It appeared as though the dead man had somehow become impaled on the post, slid its twenty foot length and come to rest on the ten foot high horizontal crossbar. It was as messy as it was unbelievable.

The law official turned. 'Thank Christ you're here.' Bakerman looked pale and distinctly shaken. 'I never thought I'd be pleased to see the Feds, but I'll freely admit this has got me rattled. I mean, unless he's been dropped out of a helicopter or something I don't see how he got there.'

Dawson walked over and stared up at the dead man's bloodied face. 'Any ID?'

'We haven't touched the body yet but it's no one I know. Jim Chievely, the groundskeeper, didn't recognise him either.'

'This Chievely, he found the body, yes?'

Bakerman nodded. 'He called us out first thing this morning and we came over straight away. I don't know what to make of it. I've seen plenty of shootings, stabbings and traffic accidents, but nothing like this.'

'You must have called the Bureau pretty quickly . . . ' Dawson raised an eyebrow questioningly. It was extremely rare for them to be asked to help from the very beginning of a case.

Bakerman looked slightly embarrassed. 'Well, you see we've got a big weekend coming up. Two of the college teams are playing a fundraiser here in a couple of days' time. It's been planned for months. I'm already under pressure to clear this up so that the game can go ahead.'

'Who's applying the pressure?'

'Cal Bryant. He's the top businessman in town. He owns the sports complex and set all of it up. It's a really big deal for him and word is he's looking to get into politics; you know the type? Doing charity work looks good, plus he runs the food concessions for the games and we're expecting a *lot* of people.' Bakerman gave

Dawson a meaningful look. 'He wants the deceased out of here and everything smoothed over nice and quick. Now, I'm not against that in principal but only if the investigation is carried out properly.'

'Do you think he's got something to hide?'

'I wouldn't think so,' Bakerman answered. 'All Bryant cares about is making a success of the game. He just wants this problem to go away, which, given the money he's got invested in it, is understandable. This is as much his problem as ours.'

'Noted,' Dawson said. 'I take it you've photographed the scene?'

'Sure have. The prints are being developed as we speak.'

'Good. Then I suggest we bring the body down. I've seen it in situ and there's not much more we can do with it stuck there.' Dawson looked up at the corpse, momentarily lost in thought as to what was the best means of extricating it. 'I guess we'll have to dismantle the post.'

'Bryant would blow his top! Anyway, we've got a cherry picker parked over there to get him down. Undignified I guess but practical. Chievely keeps one for stand repairs and fixing the floodlights.'

After Dawson had given his approval, he waited as the pensionable, yet sprightly groundskeeper emerged from the mist and drove the cherry picker into position. Dutifully, Bakerman and his deputy then climbed aboard and were soon raised high into the air, awkwardly supporting and lifting the corpse as they went, leaving more bloodstains behind.

There was a final, obscene squelch as the body was lifted from the post.

'Okay. Bring us down. Slowly!' Bakerman shouted.

Shifting levers, Chievely lowered the aerial work platform, returning the two men and their gruesome burden to the ground.

Dawson regarded the corpse with interest, noting, with some disgust, the large, gaping hole in the abdomen. Methodically, he began to search it for clues. In an inner jacket pocket, he found a wallet, inside which was a driver's licence. 'James Hansby,' he said, reading the name out.

13

'I've never heard of him,' commented Bakerman. 'Anyway, whoever he is, how in God's name did he get up there? I mean, I don't know whether this is suicide, an accident or murder.'

'I think we can confidently rule out suicide,' Dawson said, drily. 'Even if we'd found a ladder, I fail to see how this could be self-inflicted. He's either come down on that goalpost from a consider-able height or the body's been moved there after death.' He looked over at the cherry picker. If it was possible to remove the corpse that way it was equally possible it had been placed there in a similar manner. However, he had noticed that there were no tracks visible next to the goalpost when he had arrived and yet the manoeuvring required to retrieve the corpse left obvious marks on the pitch. 'I take it the cherry picker remains on site?'

'Sure does,' Chievely replied. 'I'm hardly likely to take it home.'

'What if the killer used a spare goalpost and stuck the body on it before putting it in place?' the deputy said eagerly. 'It's a possibility,' he added, shrugging his thin shoulders at the others' sceptical looks.

'That's the dumbest thing I've ever heard,' commented Bakerman angrily. 'What kind of maniac would go to such lengths?'

'Quite possibly the kind of maniac we're dealing with,' Dawson said.

★　★　★

Now that it was early afternoon, the chill fog had lifted and the late August weather was sunny, enabling Dawson to get a proper measure of Huntersville. The town was medium-sized and well-established, some of its grander buildings being at least a hundred years old and from his hotel window he could see a pleasant, leafy park area surrounded by prosperous shops and houses. Not a bad place to visit, he reflected, but not a good place to die — certainly not in the manner that James Hansby had. The preliminary autopsy report, which had been expeditiously produced, revealed nothing of real significance; only that death had resulted from forceful impalement and probably took place sometime between midnight and six o'clock in the morning. An accompanying note from the Medical Examiner had indicated that he might be able to fix the time more accurately if the last meal of the deceased was known but, bearing in mind the massive intestinal damage, nothing could be guaranteed. There was no evidence to suggest that Hansby had died prior to his impalement. There were no traces of drugs in the body, nor any signs of a natural death. There was a complete lack of forensic evidence relating to any kind of struggle. Similarly, there was nothing noteworthy about the wrecked car other than that it was registered to the victim and was completely out of gas. Everything pointed to this being a potentially unsolvable case and he wondered whether McMasters had assigned it to him as a rebuke over his handling of the Dupont affair.

Dawson had left the unsavoury task of informing next of kin to the local law enforcement officers who had in turn handed the job to the LAPD as soon as they had found out that the deceased had lived in Los Angeles. Several phone calls to the Bureau had established that Hansby had most recently worked as a Floor Manager for several television companies and was unmarried with no close family. Checking his watch, he saw that it was coming up on two o'clock — the time he had arranged to meet up with Sheriff Bakerman and Cal Bryant in the hotel lobby.

Going to the bathroom, he examined his reflection in the mirror over the sink. A calm, self-assured, clean-shaven face looked back at him. The first hints of grey had started to appear at his temples, stark against his otherwise jet black, neatly combed hair. A past girlfriend had likened him to Robert Vaughan, although he himself never saw the resemblance. Straightening his tie, he collected his jacket from the bedroom, locked the door behind him and went downstairs and into the lobby. There were several people in the large, modern room but he immediately spotted Bakerman in an out-of-the-way corner, in the company of an equally thickset man with a large Stetson, an eye-catching, ginger handlebar moustache and an expensive taste in clothes. The man's jacket alone must have cost several hundred dollars. His initial impression was that Bryant, assuming this was he, was a Texan oil tycoon, or at least wanted to look like one.

Bakerman waved Dawson over.

'Ah, so you're the Fed. Pleased to meet you, son,' the man with the Stetson drawled.

'Agent Dawson, this is Cal Bryant, the owner of the stadium,' said Bakerman.

'Thank you for coming over, Mr Bryant.' Dawson shook hands with the business-man and took a seat. 'I realise you're a busy man and believe me, I want this incident dealt with as soon as possible.'

'Just what I like to hear.' Bryant raised a hand to the nearby barman. 'Can I indulge you in a drop of *Old Kentucky*, Agent Dawson?'

'Thank you, but no,' Dawson answered politely.

Bryant raised an eyebrow. 'A clear thinker? I can respect that. You won't mind if I have one? I've got a terrible picture in my head of that man's body.

Not wanting to sound disrespectful but I guess it must've looked like a lump of prime beef on a barbecue skewer.' He shook his head, disgusted with his own imagery. 'Mighty glad I didn't see it.'

Dawson wondered about that. As a reasonable judge of character, there did seem to be some sincerity in the man's words but the body *had* been found on his property and it was entirely possible that he was involved. Could it be that this desire to speed up the investigation was to encourage a less than thorough job?

Bryant's drink arrived and he took an appreciative sip. 'I understand that Sheriff Bakerman has told you I've got a big game coming up this weekend. The *Huntersville Hornets* are taking on the *Coyote Creek Crusaders* and believe me it's going to be a sell-out. The biggest game of the year! I've got some really important people coming along; Billy-Bob Marshall, Harry Montana, Glen Adams and Mary-Lou Snyder. You know, the Country singer? She's coming over from Nashville as a personal favour to me.'

'I understand your predicament,' replied

Dawson. 'At the moment, I see no reason why the game can't go ahead.'

'Glad to hear that.' Bryant leant forward and fixed Dawson with a steely gaze. 'I'm also very keen to avoid any negative publicity that might arise from this unfortunate incident.'

'So far, the only people who know about it are the appropriate authorities, your groundsman and you yourself,' Bakerman pointed out.

'Well, can we keep it that way, at least until after the weekend?' asked Bryant.

Bakerman looked questioningly at Dawson who nodded in tacit agreement.

'My investigations do not, at this stage, require publicity. I certainly don't see the value of bringing in the press. It's only likely to complicate things,' Dawson said.

'*Complicate things!* I'll say,' Bryant exclaimed. 'And how, in God's name, do you suppose he ended up there in the first place? I mean, I don't suppose he was shot out of a cannon or something.'

'We're working on several theories,' answered Bakerman evasively.

'Oh? Like what?' Bryant took another

sip from his drink.

There was a moment's silence.

'As I'm sure you can appreciate, this is not a straightforward death — ' Dawson began.

'Sure as hell it's not,' Bryant interrupted. 'I mean, what was it exactly? An accident, a murder?'

'I can't answer that at this stage,' Dawson said mildly. 'Do you have any enemies, Mr Bryant; anyone who might have a reason to sabotage your plans?' He realised that this was a long shot, more so when one considered the fact that the dead man hailed from Los Angeles. It seemed to him that the very public nature of Hansby's resting place was more coincidental than planned. The fact that the deceased's car had run out of gas and off the road where it had, leant weight to that supposition.

'No one at all,' Bryant answered.

Bakerman gave him a slightly sceptical look.

'Okay, I may have ruffled a few feathers over the years,' Bryant admitted. 'But I honestly can't think of anyone who would feel that aggrieved.'

Dawson decided to take Bryant's claim at face value, secure in the knowledge that the Bureau could easily find out if the man was lying. 'I've read his statement but I'd like to know a bit more about Jim Chievely, seeing as he found the body.'

Bryant shook his head. 'Now, I know that whoever finds a body gets suspected, but I can tell you, Jim is a straight-up guy. I've known him for over thirty years. He's not the brightest spark but there's not a bad streak in him. He did just what he should have and called the cops, then he got in touch with me. I wanted to go and see him but Bakerman here wouldn't let me on site.'

'We had to keep the scene of the potential crime as uncontaminated as possible. I'm sure Agent Dawson under-stands,' Bakerman commented.

'Absolutely, Sheriff. It was all done by the book,' Dawson backed him up. He turned his attention to Bryant once more. 'As a precaution, I'd advise you to have extra security measures around the stadium for the next few days. You should also understand that if I deem it necessary, we will require full access to the area.'

'Okay, that sounds reasonable, I guess.' Bryant nodded. 'And you'll keep me in the loop, I hope?'

'Of course, Mr Bryant.' Dawson decided that the conversation was not going to elicit any further information. He stood up and said his goodbyes. Walking back towards the elevator, he was hailed by one of the receptionists at the front desk. She had a note from headquarters asking him to call at his earliest convenience. Returning upstairs, he dialled the number and was unsurprised when he was put through to Special Agent Dean.

'Dawson. Got some info on Hansby that you might find interesting.'

'Go on.'

'It appears that he had worked on several TV shows, all in Los Angeles. One was an afternoon cookery show; another was that programme about people who get their pets married in Vegas. No obvious leads there, but what might be important is the fact that, according to the janitor at the apartment he owned, Hansby had recently improved the security at his home. *Significantly* improved it. We're talking security cameras and heavy-duty bolts. Hell, he even had two Rottweilers for Christ's sake! It appears that something, or someone, had him really spooked.'

2

Stoker

Four days had passed since the discovery of James Hansby. Bryant's football game had gone ahead without disruption and the local press had been successfully kept in the dark. Unfortunately, Dawson felt like he was still in the dark too. No further leads had come to light in Huntersville and the deceased's Los Angeles apartment had yielded no clues, other than the fact that there was an inordinate level of recently installed security. The two guard dogs had been found alive and well and would be rehomed. Whatever Hansby's fears were it seemed he had not confided them to anyone else, at least, no one had come forward. His dash from Los Angeles to Huntersville had been traced by several speed cameras that had clocked him driving well in excess of the limit.

Interestingly, the cameras also recorded a black Ford Maverick which could conceivably have been following him. The number plate turned out to be from a car that had been stolen earlier that day from a Los Angeles suburb and the face of the driver was far too indistinct for a positive identification. Currently the search for the car was still on.

McMasters had asked for an update on the investigation so Dawson took his slim file of evidence to the Deputy Director's office.

'So, Dawson. Apart from one skewered TV man, what have you got?' McMasters asked.

'Not much so far, I'm afraid, sir,' Dawson answered, opening his file. 'The deceased was definitely in fear of his life but I've no idea why. He does not appear to have had any enemies, nor criminal involvement; however, I strongly suspect it to be a case of murder. The question is — how was it done and who did it? There are several possibilities but they're all pretty unlikely. The fact remains that he got there . . . somehow.'

'Okay, run a possibility by me then.'

'Well, he could have been pushed out of a helicopter.'

'A helicopter?'

'Or, possibly a hot air balloon.'

'*A hot air balloon?*' McMasters sounded increasingly sceptical.

'Yes. There are several companies that operate hot air balloons within a fifty mile radius. They give scenic sightseeing rides along the coast. It's feasible that Hansby was pushed out of the basket and unfortunately fell on the post. However, this does leave us with the problem of the car which only bears Hansby's fingerprints on the steering wheel.'

'So, if I get this right, what you're suggesting is that someone pursued Hansby seventy or so miles from LA to Huntersville, where he veered off the road, conveniently close to a waiting hot air balloon that no one noticed. He was then manhandled from his vehicle, bundled into the basket and either left the balloon of his own volition, or was helped out.' McMasters shook his head. 'Dawson, you don't need me to tell you this borders on the absurd.

You'll be telling me next that someone carried him up using a jet pack.'

'I hadn't thought of that.'

McMasters sighed. 'Anything else?'

'Well, another theory is that the killer or killers used the cherry picker, placing down boards to prevent leaving tracks on the turf.'

'Okay, I could give that slightly more credence,' McMasters said, nodding.

'But that in itself is unlikely for the very reason that, even at full extension, the cherry picker does not go that much higher than the post itself. The injuries inflicted do seem to indicate that Hansby fell from some height onto the post.'

'Hmm, I see what you mean. Well, if the facts don't fit the theory, either you don't have all the facts or the theory is a bust. Of course, the stolen car might turn up, that could give us some forensic evidence if we're lucky. Something that worries me is the excessive nature of the death. The only times I've heard of anything so over the top it's been Mob-related — it sends a message; a warning to others.'

'He could, of course, have been unlucky enough to have witnessed something that he shouldn't have but even so it seems a bit heavy-handed. I have to confess that all we're doing at the moment is finding dead-ends.'

'I don't think there's much justification in pursuing this further. Obviously, we'll keep the case open but I think we'll need to hand this back to the local law enforcement team. I was hoping that this was something you could have dealt with quickly.' McMasters leant back in his chair. 'I'm not criticising you, I just think our resources would be best used elsewhere.'

Dawson grimaced. 'You might be right. However, I'm loathe to abandon the case just yet and there is someone who springs to mind who might help us. Someone who's based in LA and someone who's good at thinking outside the box . . . '

McMasters scowled, his face visibly sagging. 'You don't mean Stoker, do you?'

'He's been useful in the past.'

'Yeah, but the man's a nutcase! A loose cannon. The last I heard he was a washed out gumshoe; a bitter, barely functioning alcoholic and that's even without his dubious beliefs.' McMasters shook his head. 'I'm not happy getting him involved. Although . . . he was a good agent before he went off the rails, very good in fact.'

'One of our best,' Dawson agreed, pushing the point home. 'And it can't hurt to at least get another opinion before we give up.'

McMasters thought for a long moment, battling with uncertainty, and then he finally nodded his head. 'Alright. I'll authorise one payment for consultancy but if he doesn't come up with anything, that's it.'

'Thank you, sir. I don't think you'll regret it.'

'I damn well hope not! And for God's sake, keep this quiet. The last thing I want is for the press to get hold of this.'

'I'll be the soul of discretion.' Dawson smiled as he gathered his papers and left the office.

★   ★   ★

'I hope it's not presumptuous of me to assume that you've seen some of my performances and know that I've a certain sympathy with . . . the darker side of religion. I'd even go as far as to say that the Devil's my greatest fan. Yes, I think you'll find me more tolerant than most regarding your personal beliefs, Mr Stoker.'

'Well, that makes things easier.' Fifty-three year old private investigator Vincent Stoker was glad to hear that particular stumbling block was out of the way. Even in Los Angeles, with all its inherent weirdness, knowledge of his active participation in the Church of Lucifer tended to put a damper on things and had cost him no end of prospective clients, in addition to his career in the FBI. And yet it had not been without its own rewards. Through networking, it had enabled him to acquire the office he was now in as well as several new contacts. In addition, there was the darkly mysterious and highly attractive woman seated across from him. A woman he would guess to be in her mid-thirties. She was dressed in a black leather biker's jacket, tight denim jeans that were torn at the knees and an *Alice*

Cooper heavy metal T-shirt — the kind that was all the rage with the teenage head bangers. She also wore an outrageous amount of Satanic-inspired jewellery — a pentagram necklace, earrings and rings with demon faces and a triple six inscribed silver belt buckle.

'I take it Zack hasn't told you much about the nature of my problem?'

'He just mentioned that you might need my help.' When Zack Bugliosi, one of the newer members of the Church, had told Stoker that a female friend of his was in need of some extremely discrete assistance, he had never imagined it to be Samantha De'Carlo, femme fatale and star of dozens of late night, horror B-movies and over the top gore fest presentations. A seductive vamp, who had adopted the stage name, *Lucretia Mortis* — *Queen of the Undead* — he had seen her several times on the television, emerging from coffins or creeping through misty cemeteries whilst blatantly fake bats swirled around. Aside from the ghoulish trappings, she was a dead ringer for the silent screen idol, Louise Brookes. In addition, she had a tall, slim

32

figure that a man could dream about and a remarkably fair, milky complexion which contrasted starkly with the suntanned look of everyone else he knew.

'Good. I asked him to be as sparing with the details as possible. So, Mr Stoker, last week, I received a letter, which informed me, in no uncertain terms, that unless I stopped doing what I do I was going to be murdered.'

'Do you have the letter?' Stoker stared intently into her dark green eyes and for a brief moment he felt himself drowning, captivated, mesmerised almost. Accentuated as they were by black liner and eyeshadow, the woman's eyes possessed the lethality of tar pits, capable of holding a man and swallowing him, body and soul. Somehow, he managed to break their hold.

'No. Unfortunately I tore it up in a fit of rage.' De'Carlo reached into a jacket pocket and removed a small brown envelope. 'However, three days ago I received this.' She handed it over.

Stoker examined it briefly. There was nothing unusual about the exterior — no writing, postmarks or stamps. He opened it. Inside was a small photograph. On the obverse, it showed De'Carlo, voluptuous and elegant as ever, succubus-like, with a small pair of horns, posed, in her inimitable gothic style, one arm looped over a leering demonic idol no doubt in preparation for one of her many magazine promotions. The noticeable anomaly however was the thick red line that had been drawn, separating her head from her body. He looked at the reverse, half-expecting to find some crudely written warning but it was blank.

'At first I thought little of it,' De'Carlo revealed. 'Hell, I get hundreds of letters a week. It's junk fan mail for the main; marriage proposals, begging letters, pleas from the lonely and the desperate. A lot of it's sick and deranged and all goes to prove, to me at least, that there are far crazier people than myself out there. What I do is mostly an act, something that many of my fans fail to realise. Yet to read some of the material I get sent you'd think I was the Antichrist's mother or something.'

Stoker tapped the photograph. 'Yet clearly you think this is something far more sinister?'

'I guess I wouldn't be here if I didn't.' De'Carlo smiled.

'Okay. Let's start with the basics. Tell me a bit about yourself.'

De'Carlo paused before answering, seemingly considering what to say. 'My personal life is a little different from most. I live in a large, somewhat unusual, mansion overlooking the Hollywood Heights. Think of the house in *The Munsters* and you'll be halfway there. I don't live there alone, however. I share my place with quite a group of like-minded people. A sort of commune, if you will.'

Stoker raised an eyebrow, unsure if he had heard right. '*A commune?*'

'Yes, but . . . don't be thinking a sort of Charles Manson-style commune, or anything along those lines. These people are like my extended family.' De'Carlo paused and pursed her lips. 'Okay, maybe it does sound like Charles Manson but believe me it isn't. Rather, they're my friends and dare I call them — '

'Worshippers? Slaves?'

'No! Certainly not! Hangers-on, and I don't want to sound derogatory when I say that. We support and assist each other. We party together. We share the same worldview. Combined, we embrace a way of living that promotes a certain ideology, one that's not constrained by the rigours of modern life and what little that has to offer.'

'Sounds like a cult to me,' Stoker responded, somewhat judgementally.

'From what Zack's told me, the doctrines of the Church of Lucifer aren't that dissimilar,' De'Carlo retorted. 'I know you don't sacrifice virgins, not that you'd find many in LA, or drink goat's blood. From what little I've been told, it's more to do with personal development and self-awareness. The active promotion of the individual and the elevation of the physical body over the spiritual.'

'It's a bit more complicated than that. Anyway, do you have any known enemies?'

'There are a few people from my past who have reason to hold grudges against me. Most I'd be quick to rule out as they just wouldn't have the guts to try anything. No doubt there are one or two, maybe more, who are envious of my achievements and my wealth. There's also my old friends, the 'Bible-Bashers', who are usually only too happy to turn up and get their placards out and beat their drums wherever I go. There was a concert I was supposed to attend last month and when my car pulled up they wouldn't let me out; kept banging on the windows and calling me all kinds of lovely names. There was nothing my driver could do but get me out of there before things turned nasty. Honestly, at times like that I regret not having my flamethrower. Let them know just what it's really like to burn in Hell.'

Stoker laughed. 'Do you get a lot of trouble from them?' He was only too aware how irksome the religious fanatics could be. They had launched vociferous, and indeed violent, protest marches outside his own place of worship and had targeted many of his fellow Luciferians. There had been widespread news campaigns by the Evangelical hardliners; all purposefully seeking to dismantle and destroy belief systems not compatible with their own in a puritanically driven crusade. Religious and political pressure groups were keen to maintain the moral high ground by demonstrating their willingness to expunge anything they thought threatened the youth of America and poisoned the minds of all good thinking, decent, Christian folk.

'Oh, little things here and there. They're more of a general nuisance than anything else. But all it takes is one nut . . . some crazy bastard with an axe to grind. And, as you know, unfortunately, this city's a breeding ground for the insane. Gangs and drugs on every street corner. Combine that with the heat and the oppressiveness and you've got one of the most lethal environments known to man.'

Stoker nodded in cynical agreement.

Noticing the ashtray on the private investigator's desk, De'Carlo removed a slim, gold cigarette case from a jacket pocket and with the use of a matching lighter, lit up. She took a deep draw before blowing out a small column of smoke. 'Now, either there's something behind this threat or there isn't. And that's what I'd like you to find out.'

A couple of hours after his newest client had left; Stoker was perched on his usual seat in *The Black Oyster Bar*, chain smoking and nursing his sixth double bourbon. He was feeling maudlin and naturally enough found himself ruminating upon the tragic turn his life had taken over the past few years; his wife's and his teenage daughter's deaths as the result of a drunken driver's recklessness, the days and nights spent at the hospital watching them lose their fight for life, listening helplessly to the diminishing beeps of the ECG machines to which they were wired, the travesty of a Los Angeles' lawsuit and the brutal joke of the driver having no licence, let alone insurance.

Their deaths had been the catalyst for so many downward spirals.

A loving, comfortable and ordered

existence utterly wiped out in a split second of madness; of screeching tyres, shattered glass and tangled metal. He had known he could never return to the old way of living. Maybe it would have been better if he had been in the car with them and they had all gone together. During the dark days and darker nights that followed, he had been suicidal. And then, when everything had been at its lowest ebb and an addiction to alcohol had almost claimed him, an old friend had suggested he cast aside his casual Christianity and seek some level of succour in another faith, giving him a chance to rebuild some of the wrecked dreams which he had thought were gone forever, enabling him to at least come to terms with his painful memories and try to shape a new existence for himself.

Stoker stared into his glass, swirling the melting ice, lost for a moment in his soul-wrenching thoughts.

'Hello, Vincent.'

Surprised at hearing his name mentioned, the private investigator looked up and turned his head.

Special Agent Brett Dawson stood nearby. In one hand, he carried a slim blue folder.

Stoker's eyes narrowed. It had been over two years since they had last met and they had parted company not the best of friends.

A moment of uneasy silence passed.

Stoker fixed Dawson with an unwelcoming stare. 'What do you want?' He took a sip from his drink, relishing the burn of the raw liquor.

'I need your help.'

'*My help?*'

'That's what I said.'

'And . . . just where was your help when I needed it?' Stoker sharply countered.

'I'm sorry for whatever happened between you and — '

'Please, spare me your sympathies,' Stoker interrupted, waving a dismissive hand. 'You know as well as I do that I was the one chosen for promotion; not you, or even Wright for that matter.' He stabbed his thumb at his chest. 'But then, *I* was the one given the boot. *I* was the one that got kicked in the teeth. Thirty years of loyal, hard-working service consigned to the trash! And why? All because someone made it public knowledge that my personal beliefs aren't held to be in accordance with those expected of an upstanding member of the Bureau.'

'It wasn't just that, Vincent.'

'Don't bullshit me! Of course it was.'

'You know that I, more than anyone, put my neck out to defend your good name; your excellent record.'

'It makes no difference. I still got sent packing. No farewell party. No trial for unfair dismissal. No nothing. Just a paltry pension; a third of what I should have been entitled to. And the beauty of it all is I can't even lodge a complaint — after all, who's going to side with a Devil-worshipper?'

'You must admit, Devil-worshipping has a bit of notoriety about it. Something that doesn't sit easy in the minds of the public.'

'Thus speaks the ignorant and the unenlightened.'

'Maybe, but you can't deny the general

perception. Surely you must have realised your actions — '

'*Actions?*' Stoker raised his voice. '*What actions?* I've done nothing illegal. No doubt you'll be surprised to learn that my new belief's taught me a lot about myself; given me a new perspective on coping with all the crap that life tends to throw at you, something which my previous religion failed to provide. It's given me an inner strength; an ability to better myself without slavishly adhering to a dogma which seeks to deny the individual contentment and ultimate happiness.'

Dawson cast a disapproving eye around the squalid bar with its gathered, semi-drunk disreputable and shifty-looking patrons. Fortunately, none of them seemed interested in their conversation. 'And . . . *are* you happy?'

'Yeah, of course I'm happy,' Stoker snapped. 'What makes you think otherwise?' He finished his drink and signalled to the barman for another.

'We go back a long way, Vincent. We used to be friends. It doesn't take a genius to see that things aren't going well for you. Believe me, I know things have been hard for you — losing Annie and Elizabeth and then your job, and while I can't turn the clock back, I can help you if you're prepared to help me.'

'Sounds as though you're after my soul. Too late. I'm afraid that's been offered to another. And actually, I'm doing pretty well now.'

'I'm appealing to the man I knew five years ago. One of the finest agents there ever was.'

'I'm afraid you're wasting your time,' replied Stoker coldly. Reaching into a pocket, he removed a couple of crumpled dollar bills and paid for his drink.

'Look, Vincent. I've not come here to beg, but I really could do with your help.'

'And just what would your boss think? Surely you're not here behind his back.'

'Times have changed, Vincent. McMasters is in charge now and he's the one who has authorised this meeting.'

'Old 'Bald Eagle' is in charge is he? Well, that does surprise me.' Stoker allowed himself to relax a fraction. Of all his former work colleagues the man stood before him had without doubt been his favourite. A man whom he had been able to have a friendly chat with and who had been genuinely tolerant of his beliefs. Unlike the majority, who upon learning of his presumed diabolical pursuits, had been quick to castigate and ridicule him; muttering snide comments behind his back and baaing like goats whenever they passed by.

'So what do you say? Will you help? I've been driving all day just to ask you and finding you wasn't that easy either.'

'If I do, what's in it for me? I mean, let's face it, it's not as if you can get me reinstated, not that I'd want you to anyway.'

'I'll see to it that you're paid . . . and paid well.'

'*Money?*' Stoker was surprised. A financial reward was not something he had considered.

'A consultancy fee to start with at least and more if we get somewhere.'

'How much?'

'Enough. The rates have gone up since your time.' Dawson placed the folder on the bar. 'This contains all the information we have. If you'd just take a look. I'll freely admit, it . . . doesn't make any sense to me.'

Stoker's eyes flickered to the folder. 'I might get round to it.' He ran a hand down his unshaven chin and then took a drink from his glass.

'Okay.' Dawson nodded. 'It's been good seeing you again, Vincent. I hope you decide to get in touch. You know how to contact me.' He gave a brusque nod, headed for the door and left.

★ ★ ★

Stoker had sobered up slightly by the time he got back to his modest apartment, a twenty minute walk from the bar. He had stopped off at a greasy late night diner for a burger en route and there was an unpleasant burning in his guts. He went up the darkened stairway, along the communal landing, unlocked his door and placed the folder on a table before going into the bathroom and fixing himself a glass of *Stomach-Eaze*. Taking the folder into his cluttered study, he opened it up and began looking through it.

It was the photographs that initially drew his attention.

The slumped figure, hanging over the goalpost crossbar, looked almost comical at first, like a ragdoll, until he noticed the red smears running the length of the upright. It reminded him of an image he had seen of the Devil holding aloft his pitchfork, a naked sinner transfixed on one of its prongs and for a fleeting moment he wondered if this was how he was going to end up. The second photograph had obviously been taken during the autopsy and the sizeable hole in the corpse's abdomen was clearly visible. He read through the accompanying notes, making a few of his own, and had to admit that, on the face of it, it posed certain problems. He did, at least, agree with Dawson's deduction that it had to be murder. He was half-inclined to ditch it, to concentrate on De'Carlo's problem, aware of the difficulties involved in running two cases simultaneously.

Outside, on the street, came the sound

of sirens — the never-ending night music of the City of Angels.

In the course of his work as a private investigator, Stoker had been exposed to murkier depths than he had encountered during his time in the FBI and something about Hansby's death felt vaguely familiar. The link was proving elusive, as though the more he thought about it, the more it slipped away. He stood up and moved over to the window. The night was illuminated by the many streetlamps and neon signs that never seemed to be turned off. Staring out over the city, he realised his mind was already made up. Despite his disinclination to work for the Bureau ever again, the Hansby case was too intriguing to ignore.

3

From Riches to Rags

The next morning found Stoker going through the many files and notes he had accumulated on past investigations; searching for anything that might be of use. It was proving futile, so he decided to focus his attention on delving deeper into Hansby's background. From the notes, he learned that Dawson had ascertained the two television programmes that Hansby had been working on prior to his death and a little digging showed that they had been produced by the same company — *Sunrise Productions*. Aware that the Bureau had probably interviewed the producer of the shows, but come up with nothing, he decided to go further down the chain of command. The head office was not far away and he set off to see what he could find.

Sunrise Productions was housed in a large building in downtown Los Angeles.

The lobby had been decorated with various promotional images from the numerous television shows the company produced. The receptionist on duty was suitably impressed at meeting a private investigator — especially one who was ruggedly handsome in a sort of world-weary way — and proved happy to gossip.

'Mr Hansby? James Hansby? You say he's dead! That's terrible news. Although, I have to admit, I had a feeling that something was wrong. There were some cops here just a few days ago but the boss didn't want to tell us anything.' The woman was clearly shocked but not grief-stricken. 'He never appeared in the best of health you know. Kind of grey and worried. Tired-looking, as though he wasn't getting enough sleep.'

Failing to correct the woman's assumption that Hansby had died of natural causes, Stoker encouraged her to talk. 'What was he like?'

'He'd only been on the payroll for about a month or so and he never really said much to me. Kept himself to himself you could say. Like I said, he was a bit nervy; highly-strung.'

Stoker lit a cigarette and took a deep drag. 'What makes you say that?'

'It's hard to say really, but there were little things. Like, he always checked the street before he left the building and a couple of times he would leave by the back door as if he was trying to get away unnoticed. He had a sort of constantly wary look about him . . . as though he'd just walked under a ladder and was expecting something bad to happen.' The receptionist shrugged. 'Whatever it was, he didn't last here long. I was told he resigned about three weeks ago.'

'Any idea why?'

'I'm afraid not. You should really talk to Jerry Mansfield. He worked with Mr Hansby a lot, but he's filming over in Colorado for the next week or so.'

'Do you have a number for him?'

'Sorry, no. They're making a documentary on Indian reservations and he's moving around a lot. It's possible he might call in, I guess.'

'If he does, can you please give him my number?' Stoker handed the woman his business card.

'Sure.' The receptionist paused uncertainly. 'I don't want to sound nosey but, why are you asking about all this? Didn't Mr Hansby just have a heart attack or something?'

'There are a couple of questions about his death, that's all,' Stoker said calmly. Dawson had not specified secrecy but had strongly hinted that, certainly for the time being, the Bureau preferred to keep the exact details of the victim's demise out of the public domain. 'Thanks for your time.' He turned to leave but a series of posters on the wall caught his eye. *Sunrise Productions* had recently finished a set of educational television programmes on some of the more gruesome aspects of history — European Medieval torture, the Spanish Inquisition, the Salem Witchcraft Trials and Vlad the Impaler. The latter elicited a wry smile. It was ghoulishly apposite to his investigation of the unfortunate Hansby.

★   ★   ★

Shaking his head in disbelief, Stoker glanced briefly at the large stone gargoyle perched atop the gate post outside the De'Carlo mansion. A sturdy wooden gate prevented any inquisitive eyes from seeing through into the grounds. He pressed the intercom buzzer, looked up, smiled at the security camera and waited. A few moments later the gate drew back and he entered.

A long, meandering driveway wound among well-kept but unusual gardens. A distinctly graveyard theme was apparent with mock headstones, an artfully decaying summerhouse and weeping birch trees lining the paths. Creepy-looking statues peopled the otherwise deserted gardens.

The house which loomed over its surroundings lived up to Stoker's expectations.

Late eighteenth century in style, with a veranda, gothic windows, two turrets and enough decorative iron railings to build a warship. It was impressively large, even for the Hollywood Heights and the views from its top windows would be breath taking. The overall theme was highly theatrical and more than a little hammy.

The effect was slightly spoilt by the

bright, Los Angeles sunshine. It would be far better on a dark, storm-ravaged night; the rain falling heavily and the structure lit up against the blackness by flashes of lightning.

Stoker could not help admiring it. Had he the money it was the kind of place he would like to own. It would be ideal for throwing Halloween parties. He climbed the few steps to the veranda and saw the lady of the house waiting for him in the doorway. She was attired more normally this time in a dark green cotton dress, slim sandals and a sunhat — preserving her pale skin from the sun.

Smiling, De'Carlo greeted her visitor. 'What do you think of my humble abode?'

'Impressive. It reminds me of a film set. Like the house from *Psycho*.'

'I'll let you into a little secret. Parts of it are exactly that. I know a few props managers and they send things my way from time to time. The gravestones were designed for the 1935 Tod Browning film *Mark of the Vampire*. That is, except for old Ezekiel Waite's.' De'Carlo gestured to one corner of the garden. 'He was the original owner of the house and I didn't have the heart to move him. Anyway, why don't you come in?' She turned and led the way inside.

To Stoker's surprise, the interior was markedly different from the exterior. He had expected the gothic theme to be continued; suits of plate mail, dripping candlesticks and a sweeping staircase, complete with sinister portraits and swathes of cobwebs. In actual fact, the house was clean, light, relatively modern and tastefully furnished.

'You realise you can't leave now you know my secret. I'm only a fake freak.'

'Aren't most people?' Stoker replied. 'Except for the occasional obsessive we're all pretty much the same.'

'Talking of obsessives, come and meet the rest of us.' De'Carlo led the private investigator along a corridor, past a room in which two men were playing pool and opened a door into a large conservatory where a dozen or so other people had clearly just finished eating lunch. They were an assorted bunch of men and women, ranging in age from early twenties right up to a grizzled sixty-something who regarded the newcomer with some suspicion. 'Everyone. This is Vincent Stoker; a friendly Satanist who I'm hoping can help me with that little problem we've spoken about.'

Stoker winced inwardly at the introduction. He did not like his beliefs being so publicly proclaimed, more so when they were, strictly speaking, incorrect. Though, judging from the response from the room, this group did not hold the usual prejudices. There were some interested looks and one or two understanding nods but no signs of disapproval.

'Wolf, Maureen. Could you join me in the study, please?' The older, bearded man and a slightly plump, homely-looking woman got to their feet and, along with Stoker, followed De'Carlo into a smaller room off the conservatory.

Stoker took in the decoration with interest. Promotional pictures of De'Carlo as *Lucretia Mortis* covered the walls. The room also contained professional-looking filing cabinets, two mahogany desks with a typewriter and a telephone on each and a few chairs. He considered the ill-matched trio as they all took their seats round a circular table by the window. Maureen strongly reminded him of his sole remaining aunt; motherly and conservatively dressed. The only unusual thing he could see was a silver bat necklace she wore on a black cord. Wolf, on the other hand, was probably a Hell's Angel, or had been in his younger years. Faded, yet still visible *Love* and *Hate* tattoos adorned his knuckles and he wore a shark's tooth earring. His skin had been burned a deep mahogany from years spent motor biking along desert, cacti-lined, sun-scorched highways. The potentially aggressive appearance was tempered by his paunch, his grey hair and the rugged lines on his face which indicated a more avuncular demeanour.

'I've explained to Vincent about the death threat and the photograph,' said De'Carlo. 'He's agreed to look into it for me.'

'Good! The sooner we find out which bastard did this, the better.' Wolf scratched at his beard. 'I won't rest easy till then.'

Maureen nodded her head in agreement. 'Yes, I really do think it's time to sort this out. I can't believe anyone would actually hurt you, Samantha, but we can't be too careful.'

'Mr Stoker, meet my mom and pop.' De'Carlo smiled. 'Not my real ones of course. Being Mormons, they don't exactly approve of my way of life. Wolf is my manager, driver and all round minder. Maureen . . . what would you say that you do?'

'You mean apart from everything?' Maureen remarked. 'I cook, I clean, I pay the bills, feed the cats and provide a shoulder to cry on when tempers fray. And what's more, I don't get paid for it.'

'You see? Mom and pop,' De'Carlo said fondly. 'These two have looked after me for over ten years.'

'Can you give me your take on the threatening letter?' Stoker addressed Wolf.

'It arrived in the mail last week and Maureen opened it, as she does with all Samantha's correspondence. As you can probably appreciate, she gets a lot of rubbish and Maureen goes through it all to check for anything important and to sort out the fan mail.' Wolf reached into a jacket pocket, took out a small, half-empty bottle of Jack Daniel's and took a swig.

'We get some strange stuff, that's true, but nothing like this,' Maureen said. 'I went straight to find Wolf.'

'And then we got together with Samantha. I wanted to call the police but she thought we should just ignore it,' Wolf said, frowning.

'I was sure it was nothing. Unpleasant, but not a real problem.' De'Carlo sounded slightly defensive. 'Then the photograph turned up.'

Wolf's face darkened. 'That was when I put my foot down. I told Samantha she had to get some proper advice. We're doing a complete overhaul of the security systems too but that's no guarantee of safety. Just look at what happened to Larry Hamilton over in Beverly Hills. He had a state of the art surveillance system — the best that money can buy, plus bodyguards, and it didn't do him any good. Poor bastard.'

'Can you fill in a few gaps for me here?' Stoker asked questioningly. 'Who's Larry Hamilton?'

'You haven't heard about it?' Maureen queried, incredulously.

'You're forgetting, we only heard about it ourselves yesterday and it hasn't hit the papers yet,' De'Carlo said. 'Larry Hamilton was a TV producer. I worked with him a few times on this and that. Well, something happened to him a couple of days ago. The rumour is that he was killed in his garden and no one can work out how it happened. The only thing that's certain is he's dead.'

'The last thing we need is another Manson on the loose. These crazy bastards want notoriety from targeting famous folk,' Wolf growled.

'I can see how that would worry you,' Stoker agreed. 'I'd certainly advise you to be very careful regarding security for the moment. You could also ask for police protection. I can tell you who best to contact, while I look into the 'who and why' aspect of this. What I really need from you now is details of anyone who might bear you a grudge. If this isn't some random nutcase then there'll be a clue somewhere. I'd also like to see a sample of your fan mail; to get an idea of what your normal correspondence is like.' He paused, wondering how to word his next request. 'I'd also like to get a bit of information on everyone who lives here, including anyone who may have left recently.'

'Surely you don't suspect any of my friends?' De'Carlo was surprised.

'Not for any particular reason, at the moment,' Stoker answered. 'According to statistics, however, a large percentage of hate mail crimes are committed by people known to the victim so I can't ignore the possibility and neither should you.'

'Personally, I think this has come from outside,' Wolf said.

'I'd like to hope so, but we can't ignore the possibility,' Maureen countered. 'Why don't I tell you a bit about us all?'

Stoker found the next half hour certainly enlightening, if overwhelming.

Over a cup of coffee brought by one of the household, Maureen outlined the histories of all of the residents, including some who had moved on.

Wolf and De'Carlo also contributed

their views and the private investigator wrote copious notes. He was grateful for the information but after a while he found his mind drifting back to the photograph of James Hansby, skewered on the goal post. *How the hell was it done? Why the hell was it done?* Dragging his attention back to Maureen, he found she was talking about the last resident.

' . . . and she came to us a couple of months ago. Samantha got to know her when she was working as a costumier for the theatre.'

'Thanks, I think we'll leave it there for now. You've given me more than enough to be going on with.' Stoker took his leave of them, appreciating the carefully dishevelled gardens once more and with the bizarre death of Hansby still intruding on his thoughts.

★   ★   ★

'Oh Christ!' Police Detective Chuck Lovenski exclaimed as he looked up from his mass of paperwork to see Stoker entering his office. 'What are you doing here, Vince? I distinctly remember telling you not to come back after last time.'

'Good to see you too, Chuck.' Stoker closed the door behind him, stepped in and sat down at the desk opposite his fellow Luciferian — a competent, hard-working police detective who cared more about justice than career advancement. He complained a lot and tended to slouch as though burdened by the weight of the world but, nevertheless, could be good company off-duty.

'You do realise that if certain information about me ever gets out, I'll lose my job and you'll lose your way into the LAPD?'

'Lighten up, this isn't the FBI. The LAPD will take anybody — you for example.' Stoker grinned. 'Anyway, there's no reason to be worried. I'm a registered private investigator with a perfect right to talk to my fellow crime fighters about a case. As I have in the past with no repercussions.'

'Ah, I suppose so.' Lovenski sighed.

'Besides, nobody *here* knows about me anyway.'

'Let's keep it that way, shall we?

Anyway, what do you want?'

Stoker lit a cigarette, put it between his lips and inhaled deeply. 'James Hansby? Ring any bells?'

'Hansby? The goalpost guy?'

'So the FBI told you about his unusual end. Surprising.'

'I think someone let it slip.' Lovenski leaned forward on his elbows. 'It's the kind of thing that was bound to get out sooner or later. But how do *you* know about Hansby?'

'Doing a favour for an old friend.'

'You have friends?' Lovenski raised a sceptical eyebrow.

'It must be my considerate nature,' Stoker deadpanned. 'I just want to know what you guys thought about the case, then I'll be out of your hair, or rather what's left of it.' He crossed his arms. 'You know, you're looking more and more like *Kojak* every time I see you.'

Lovenski sighed audibly and shook his head in exasperation. 'Okay, Vince. But you owe me. The next few drinks at least.'

'Sounds like a deal.'

'I wasn't part of the team on that case

but it was pretty routine, apart from the corpse of course. Bennet and Carson tried to find next of kin and they checked out his flat but came up with nothing.'

'So I've heard. How about the car that was tailing him out of the city?'

'You *have* done your homework. That turned up yesterday. I would've heard if anything useful has come of it so I wouldn't expect anything there. To be honest, I think the whole case is a dead-end.'

'Maybe. Maybe not. Someone, somewhere must know something. For example, where did the vehicle turn up?' Stoker inquired.

'Hmm, not sure. Somewhere on Skid Row, I think. If anyone saw something there, they're not telling us.'

'Yeah, but they might tell me. Get me that location, Chuck and I'll stand you a steak dinner as well as the drinks. Might even put in a few good words for you.'

Lovenski made a call to a colleague and they chatted while waiting for a reply.

After inquiring about a few mutual friends, Stoker remembered the rumour that he had heard at De'Carlo's mansion. 'That's a thing, Chuck, has there been a murder in Beverly Hills — a Larry Hamilton?'

'How the hell do you know about that?' Lovenski looked utterly surprised.

'I have my sources. So what gives?'

'You're unreal, you know that? Well, I don't know much about that one. Just that some rich TV producer got himself killed in his garden, despite the place being like Fort Knox. They found him stuck under a stone fountain — just his feet sticking out. Can you believe it!?'

Stoker grimaced. 'Messy clear-up,' he commented.

'Sure was.' The telephone rang and Lovenski answered it. Putting the receiver down a moment later, he handed over a piece of paper with an address on it. 'That's where the car was found. Now get out of my office.'

'Thanks, Chuck.' Stoker got up to leave.

'Don't forget about my drinks . . . and my steak!'

'Wouldn't dream of it,' Stoker said. 'See you around.' Nonchalantly, he raised his left hand in the sign of the Fallen One and left the office.

★ ★ ★

In the City of Angels there were many places where even angels feared to tread, at least after dark. Fortunately, however, Stoker no longer believed in such heavenly protection and trod wherever he damn well liked, his private sense of security undoubtedly bolstered by the .45 automatic he kept in a concealed holster — some habits from the Bureau died hard. Turning up the collar of his coat, he stalked the streets surrounding the area where the car had been found in a search for potential witnesses. With each step, his surroundings became increasingly derelict and threatening. This was a foreboding, heavily built-up area that attracted some of the worst of human society. All manner of lawlessness took place here.

As dusk fell, the marginally more affluent residents retreated to their homes and, like ghouls, the other denizens of Skid Row started to populate the run-down streets. These were the pitiful, impoverished and occasionally dangerous lowlifes; those who through misfortune or

67

misdeeds had ended up at the bottom of the heap. Bums, drunks, whores and outcasts — shadowy figures, miserable figures; individuals whose pure existence was one of day-to-day survival. Many were high on drugs or cheap alcohol and the very air seemed to be polluted with a reek of despair. Piles of stinking garbage littered the back alleys and graffiti covered the decrepit buildings. Various hotspots arose where folk congregated — the liquor stores, the soup kitchens, and other, more furtive areas.

Stoker could see one such untidy and ragged gathering. Two vagrants were arguing over the remaining dregs in a bottle of whisky, whilst a third was rummaging through an overflowing trashcan. A mangy dog drifted down the sidewalk on its nocturnal hunt for the large rats that abounded here. The private investigator found himself briefly reflecting on the fact that his profession brought him into contact with the extremes of life in Los Angeles. Only that morning, he had visited the luxurious and undoubtedly expensive De'Carlo mansion; a place designed to duplicate the fantasy horror of the Hollywood B-movies. Now, here he was, walking the streets of a world that would *truly* strike fear into the hearts of many — the stark contrast was almost overwhelming; geographically, it was only a matter of miles separating the two yet it really was a case of Heaven and Hell.

Only a few months ago, this neighbourhood had been terrorised by Vaughan Greenwood, the so-called 'Skid Row Slasher', who had murdered at least eleven down-and-outs, slitting their throats and ritualistically leaving salt and cups of blood around the bodies.

It was the kind of thing that gave devil-worshippers a bad name.

Hands in pockets, Stoker headed over to the group, his face grim. 'Hi fellas, how'd you like to earn a dollar or two?'

'Doin' what?' came the suspicious reply from one of the men — a wizened, largely toothless black man with frazzled hair and but one good eye.

'I need some information, that's all,' said Stoker.

Draining the last drops from the bottle

which he had finally wrested from his opponent, the second hobo — a malodourous wretch in a ripped string vest, his face almost fully covered with dirt and bristling grey hair — staggered forward. Swaying slightly, he looked vaguely in Stoker's direction. 'What . . . what're you talkin' about?'

'A car was abandoned here a day or two ago — a black Ford Maverick. I'm hoping that someone saw whoever got out of it.'

'A lot of cars get dumped here. What's so special about this one?' the hirsute tramp asked.

'It might have had a killer in it,' Stoker said.

'*A killer?*' The toothless drunk shambled backwards a couple of steps. 'Tell ya somethin', *you* look like a killer mister. Maybe it was *your* car. Yeah, get outta here!' He waved his arms ineffectually.

Realising that he was unlikely to get any useful information from these two, Stoker was about to move on when he heard the click of a switchblade behind him. Spinning round, he saw an angular, scrawny young man with black hair and a bad case of acne. He was holding a small but sharp knife and was clearly high on something.

'Give me your money,' the youth snarled.

'Why should I?' Stoker asked calmly.

'Cause I'll make you bleed if you don't!'

'Is that so?' Stepping forward, Stoker drove in a hefty right punch which caught the youth smack on the chin; its numbing effect sufficient to send him sprawling to the ground, arms out flung. Kicking the dropped weapon clear, he then caught the other by the hair, dragged his head up and stared down mercilessly into the would-be mugger's unpleasant face. The eyes flickered open a few seconds later, stared up into his for a little while with no expression in them whatsoever. Then the lips drew back in a snarl as the punk sucked in a shuddering breath. He tried feebly to struggle to his feet, but the private investigator held him there with a tight grip and then thrust the barrel of his .45 hard against the underside of the

71

young man's chin. 'Now, what's stopping me from blowing your brains out, sonny?'

'Christ man! Keep it cool. I didn't — '

'Shut up! I'll do the talking.'

Upon seeing the gun, the two tramps Stoker had been talking to fled the scene. The third, the bin-diver — an almost feral-looking female with unsightly scabs and long grey hair — rushed over. 'Hey mister, you don't have to do that. Billy didn't mean you any harm,' she cried.

'You know this loser?' Stoker asked. Violently, he threw Billy against a wall. His victim struck the coarse bricks head-on and crumpled to the ground once more. 'I'll let you off this time, *if* you can help me.'

'But . . . but — ' the youth stammered, blood leaking from between the fingers clamped to his face.

'Is it about that car you were asking about?' the woman interrupted.

'Yes. Do you know anything?' said Stoker.

'Not me, and Billy's no use to anyone. You should ask Groucho. He hangs around that intersection most of the time.' The female vagrant waved her hand vaguely down the street and helped the terrified Billy up from the sidewalk. 'He sees everything that goes on here.'

'*Groucho?*' Stoker asked. 'As in Marx?'

'No, like the dude who lives in the trashcan on *Sesame Street*.' Billy dabbed at the nasty-looking gash on his forehead. 'You'll find him up by the Mission this time of night.'

'Thanks.' Stoker handed a few dollars to the woman, then turned and glanced disdainfully at Billy, who flinched. Returning his gun to his holster, he walked the short distance to the Mission, which was busy by this time, inside and out. Groucho was not difficult to track down. A few questions to the volunteers doling out soup pointed him to an old, bearded, shambolic figure, squatting on the sidewalk with an unlabelled bottle in his hand. His attempts to engage the malodorous tramp in conversation got nowhere until the .45 made an appearance.

'Okay, okay! Just don't shoot me!' Groucho cowered pitifully. 'The dude with the

Maverick? Yeah, I saw him. He's crazy! You don't wanna mess with him.'

'Interesting. Tell me more.'

'I can't! He knows things. He'd find out.'

Stoker clicked off the gun's safety catch, his eyes narrowing. 'Tell me what he looks like; a name if you know it and where he went after he abandoned the car.'

The bum's rheumy eyes widened as he found himself staring down the barrel. 'I don't know his name or where he's gone. But you'd know him if you saw him. He's freaky! Skinny with long hair and weird eyes. He can do things.'

'What kind of things?'

'You won't believe me if I tell you.'

'Try me.'

Nervously, Groucho looked around, ensuring that no one else was within earshot. 'I . . . I saw him lift a dumpster clear off the ground just by pointing at it. It wasn't far from here . . . and he probably thought no one was watching, but I saw it. I swear.'

The bell that had been quietly ringing

in Stoker's mind for the last twenty-four hours began to sound louder. It would be easy to dismiss this loser as a junkie who no longer knew what was real, but the discovery of Hansby, improbably impaled on the goal post, was a hard fact. He did not believe in magic but there were certainly some who claimed that such things were possible and there had been some strange rumours going round on the street for a while that he had been vaguely aware of. It was not uncommon for such rumours to become inflated in order to empower the teller. This time, however, seemed different. The claims of telekinesis had to be false; had to be some kind of trick, but if someone *had* found a way to levitate objects then the possible connection with the positioning of Hansby's body could not be ignored. He drew in a lungful of air, regrettably getting a strong stink off his informant. The scant detail he had been given about the killing of Larry Hamilton, crushed under a garden fountain, also warranted further investigation. He regarded the foul-smelling, snivelling vagrant with more interest. 'I want to know everything you can tell me about this man, every last detail you can remember.'

4

A Famous Informant

Stoker cradled the phone between his ear and shoulder as he pulled a piece of paper closer towards himself. In his other hand, he held a slice of peanut-buttered toast; the remnant of his breakfast. 'Apparently the man who got out of the Maverick was about thirty years old, tall and scrawny with unnerving eyes and a wispy beard. I've got a mental picture of someone a bit like *Shaggy* from the *Scooby-Doo* cartoons. He wore jeans and a Mexican-styled shirt which had a low neck. I got the bum to draw it for me, to the best of his abilities. When I asked about him at the Mission, a couple of people recognised the description and could confirm that there *is* a man like that who sometimes hangs around the district. No one wanted to talk much about him and I got a strong sense of fear from them.'

'No wonder none of them seemed to know about him when the cops went in. Should I ask how you got the vagrant to talk to you?' Dawson inquired.

'Better not. Can you get this description circulated? It might turn up something.'

'Sure. It certainly gives me an excuse to stay on the case. Still, I won't be giving any of this to McMasters, not yet at least. Can you imagine how he'd react to the idea that there was a homicidal Uri Geller on the loose?'

'It's got you interested though.' It was a statement, not a question. Stoker himself was becoming increasingly intrigued.

'Certainly has, and this Hamilton death might be worth looking into as well.'

'It's a strange coincidence at the least,' Stoker agreed. 'Can you clear it with the LAPD for me to observe on the case?'

'No problem. I'll get on to that now. If it seems to be unrelated you can drop it, but if you think there's a link, I'll come over myself. Good work, Vincent.'

'It's what you're paying me for.' Stoker put the phone down.

'I can't say that I'm completely happy about this but I suppose orders are orders,' Police Detective Thomas Ford commented as, grudgingly, he unlocked the gates of Larry Hamilton's Beverley Hills mansion.

Stoker had only had to wait half an hour for Dawson to confirm that the necessary permissions had been granted. Now he took in the lavish home of the late television producer with interest. The gardens were lushly planted, with terraces and balustrades scattered around artfully. A curving swimming pool lay off to one side with sun loungers and a nearby well-stocked, Hawaiian-style bar. The house was a two-storey, whitewashed dream of a building with palm trees offering shade over cool patios. More to the point, he noticed the many, discrete yet strategically positioned security cameras.

'The body was found around here,' Ford said, leading Stoker to a path which led around the back of the house to an area with a large, ornate fountain, surrounded by statues depicting Ancient Greek gods and goddesses.

A large, circular, grassless indentation provided evidence of the original position of the water feature which was now lying haphazardly to one side with a large chunk of stone broken off.

'Do I understand that Mr Hamilton was found underneath this?' Stoker asked, somewhat incredulously. Looking closely, he could still see the red stains which even power hosing and vigorous scrubbing had failed to remove. 'Must've been a hell of a mess!'

'That goes without saying. It would appear that he'd been lying on a sun lounger listening to some music with his headphones on. Poor bastard probably didn't know what hit him. He was found squashed flat with only his feet sticking out. Like the Wicked Witch of the East, you know?'

'No ruby slippers though, I guess,' Stoker said. Crouching down, he ran a hand, appraisingly, over the stone contours. 'This thing must weigh over a ton!'

'We contacted the company who installed it and they say it's closer to two tonnes with the water in it. Not only that, it was cemented in.' Ford ran his fingers through his hair. 'I just can't make this one out. As you can see, there's no way anyone could have sneaked heavy lifting gear in here. There were a couple of Hamilton's security men stationed at the main gate and another in the house. We've interviewed them and they've nothing of interest to report, apart from hearing a loud grating sound followed by a heavy thud. They came running to investigate but there was no one, except the deceased, in sight.'

Stoker took in his immediate surroundings, scrutinising the immediate vicinity. This side of the property was relatively secluded with plenty of vegetation an intruder could hide behind. The perimeter wall was tall but not impossible to scale and there would surely be gaps where the surveillance cameras were blind. Despite the television producer's precautions, it would not take a master burglar to gain access. The means of murder — assuming this was a homicide — was far more problematic to ascertain and the parallels with Hansby's death were significant.

'You're a PI aren't you? So what exactly is your involvement with this?' Ford asked interestedly.

Stoker considered how much to divulge. 'I used to be in the FBI. An ex-colleague has asked for assistance. It's possible that there's a link between what's happened here and a death in Huntersville. A stage manager called Hansby, who lived here in the city, was discovered in equally inexplicable circumstances.'

'I heard a little about that,' Ford admitted, nodding.

'Anyway, I wouldn't be at all surprised if the FBI take this one off your hands, but I've been assigned to do a little more digging before they make their final decision. Which brings me to my next question — did Hamilton have a secretary? I need to know about his professional and personal life. See if I can establish a link between the two deaths.'

'He had a personal assistant.' Ford took

out a small, leather-backed notebook and quickly flicked through it to the relevant page. 'Harvey Gaskill, his name is. We tried to interview him yesterday but the guy was too badly shaken up. I got the impression that he and Hamilton were . . . ' The police detective looked slightly embarrassed.

'Okay. I get your drift,' Stoker commented. 'Can I have his address?'

'Sure.' Ford scribbled down an address on a fresh page of his notebook and handed it over.

★   ★   ★

It took Stoker fifteen minutes in the chaotic Los Angeles traffic to drive to Gaskill's apartment — he could probably have walked it in ten. The neighbourhood was quietly affluent, certainly not as wealthy as Beverly Hills but still select as evidenced by the well-manicured gardens, noticeable lack of litter and the expensive cars parked along the main road. It looked comfortable and tranquil; a nice place to retire. One could almost imagine a place like this being crime-free but the cynical private investigator knew that appearances could be deceptive. Surreptitiously checking that his .45 was firmly in its holster, he got out of his car and approached the attractive, low-rise building.

Gaskill answered the intercom buzzer almost immediately and let Stoker in as soon as he had stated his business.

Stoker climbed to the second storey to find a late middle-aged man waiting for him.

'Come in, please.' Gaskill ushered the private investigator quickly inside his spacious apartment.

Brightly coloured, modern paintings adorned the walls and pot plants filled the windowsills. A disinterested cat lay in a patch of sunshine and barely flicked its tail at the entrance of the stranger.

Stoker spotted several framed photographs of Gaskill with Hamilton and minor celebrities. Then he turned his attention to the man himself. The television producer's personal assistant was slightly chubby and beginning to lose his hair. He looked to be the kind of man that would usually be jovial and upbeat but the death of his employer had clearly hit him hard.

'Is there any news?' Gaskill asked intently.

'I'm afraid it's still early days but I can tell you that the FBI are taking an interest,' Stoker answered.

'Oh, thank God!' Gaskill exclaimed and sank unsteadily onto a couch. 'Mmm . . . maybe they can get to the bottom of this nnn . . . nightmare. It just seems so unreal, absolutely un . . . unbelievable! How in hell's name did it happen?' In addition to his nervous stammering, his blue eyes were red-rimmed and his hands shook noticeably.

'I think that's going to be the crux of the matter. Anything you can tell me about what prompted Mr Hamilton's recent changes to his security arrangements would be most helpful.' Stoker pulled over a chair and seated himself next to a table.

'Of course, but, please for . . . forgive me. This has been so hard for me to take in.' Gaskill reached into a pocket and removed a small pill bottle. Seeing Stoker's questioning glance, he explained. 'The ddd . . . doctor gave me these yesterday for my nerves. I suppose they might do sss . . . something but I'd much rather have a stiff brandy.'

'Sounds like a good idea to me. Can I get you one?' Stoker offered.

'You won't find any alcohol here.' Gaskill shook his head. 'I haven't ttt . . . touched a drop in over thirty years and I'm sure Laa . . . Larry wouldn't have wanted me to start again.' He unscrewed the cap of the pill bottle and managed to shake a good handful of small white tablets into the palm of his hand. Tremulously, he selected four; put them in his mouth and dry swallowed them. Pouring the rest of the pills back into the container, he took several deep breaths.

'You just take your time, Mr Gaskill.' Stoker was not usually known for his patience or tact but he could see that this interview would have to be handled delicately if he wanted to get anything useful from it. It was clear that the man was a nervous wreck. That in itself did not prove innocence for he had known several murderers who had been genuinely distraught at their actions. Others had just been actors worthy of an Oscar. 'There's no rush.'

'Well . . . I think it was about four months ago that Larry sta . . . sta . . . started to seem a little worried. He'd always kept his home secure. He had some very nice possessions and this is Los Angeles after all. But sud . . . suddenly, it wasn't enough. He wanted more cameras and he's never had bodyguards before — not that they did any good.'

'You don't think one of them killed Mr Hamilton, do you?' Stoker asked, curious to see how Gaskill would take the question.

'Of course not! I mean, why should they? He was paying them very well and the work wasn't hard.'

'Just a thought.' Stoker gently chewed his bottom lip, thinking things through. 'What about enemies? Did he have any? Perhaps someone with a grudge?'

'Clearly he had at least one!' Gaskill

blurted angrily. 'That fff . . . fountain didn't fall on him of its own accord!'

'True. But is there anyone that you know about? For instance, did he owe anyone money? Had he broken any contracts? Obviously I'm not that clued up on the business but is it possible that a man of his influence could have spoilt someone's chances of stardom?' Stoker rattled off the suggestions.

'Okay.' Gaskill took a measured breath. Undoubtedly due to the fast-acting medication, he seemed to have regained some sense of composure. 'Firstly, as Larry's personal assistant over many years I can assure you that he was financially secure and he didn't have any bad habits like gambling or drinking, or drugs for that matter. And that, I can tell you, is a rarity in this business! Just like any producer, he's had his ups and downs and on occasion we've had to withdraw from commitments but that's not unusual.' He paused, considering the last question. 'As far as I'm aware, Larry never spoilt anyone's chances. I'll admit that he could be difficult in some of his dealings and he didn't suffer fools. But it's not like his programs were make-or-break tickets to fame.'

'So what were they?'

'He did all sorts, from advertising to dramas as well as some gameshows. He also helped out on one or two of the religious channels. His greatest claim to fame however was the series of documentaries he did in the late 1960s on the, let's say, weirder inhabitants of LA.'

'Such as?'

'Well, there was his feature on the Brownson family; an inbred clan of modern-day cannibals that lived on a ranch just outside Pasadena. Believe it or not, he actually got permission to interview Sid Brownson, the last remaining member of the group. Then there was *Unreal Lives* — the half-hour series he did about people with unusual ailments or talents. People like Valarie Rhomer, the female Houdini, Ken 'Wolfman' Jackson, who claimed to be the only living individual diagnosed with lycanthropy and Martin Bliss Junior — a talented artist who paints with his own excrement.'

Stoker winced. 'Christ!'

'You can mock, but his artwork commands very high prices. I for one wouldn't say 'no' to having one of his hanging on my wall. I've been told they no longer smell, if that's what you're turning your nose up at. His studio in Santa Monica is said to be out of this world; with a generous collection of — ' Gaskill was interrupted by the sound of a phone ringing in a nearby room. Excusing himself, he got to his feet and went to answer it.

In his host's absence, Stoker found himself absently reflecting on the nature of a being who would paint using their own faeces. Was it fresh? Was it old? Were dietary requirements needed for a certain texture? How did Bliss Junior achieve different colours in his paintings, assuming that he did? These were the kind of sordid details that intrigued him and whilst he was unfamiliar with *Unreal Lives*, he was aware of several other, similar television programmes that dealt with the weird and the wonderful; delving into the many bizarre aspects of city life which, by contrast, made the Luciferian philosophy which he now lived his life by appear positively normal.

After a few minutes, Gaskill returned, a concerned look on his face. He supported himself in the doorway. 'This might be . . . relevant.'

Stoker sat up. 'What is it?'

'That was Max Chartair on the phone.'

'*Max Chartair?* As in *Chartair's Challenge?*' Stoker was surprised, for Chartair was a relatively famous, well-loved and charismatic television celebrity who had made a name for himself in the mid-1950s as a presenter for *The Huey Lambada Misfits*, *Happy Holidays* and later, the long-running cowboy-themed kids' show, *Jimmy, Grab Yer Gun*. His ratings had grown steadily throughout the 1960s when he branched out into hosting gameshows, notably *Three Ways to Get Rich; Your Face is Your Fortune* and *Diamond Dollars* as well as several light-hearted documentaries. His had been one of those faces that, only a few years ago, had seemed to be never off the television — certain channels anyway.

More recently, he had presented the paranormal investigation show, *Chartair's Challenge* — a somewhat cheesy production in which anyone who claimed to possess occult powers was invited to demonstrate their abilities and if they managed to do so under scientifically controlled conditions and to the satisfaction of the resident expert, Randall Conway, they would be awarded a hundred thousand dollar prize. No one had ever proved successful, although many had tried; spoon-benders, psychics, dowsers, mind-readers. Some had been fraudsters, yet most had been genuinely deluded. Still, it had proved to be good entertainment and had looked as though it would continue to run for years. Many participants exposed themselves to public ridicule and viewers tuned in for the jocular debunking by Conway and Chartair rather than in the expectation of seeing something amazing.

'The very same,' Gaskill answered. 'That was Larry's latest project and one he really enjoyed. He both directed and produced it. We've known Max for years and he was the obvious choice to present it — a consummate professional.'

'So, I take it he was calling with condolences?' Stoker asked.

'Well, yes but . . . he's worried. Extremely worried. Look, you're investigating this aren't you? Max was saying that James Hansby has died too. Does that mean anything to you?' Gaskill looked distinctly troubled.

The mention of Hansby sounded like a jackpot payout on a fruit machine to Stoker's ears. Here, finally, was a tangible connection. 'So, you knew Mr Hansby?'

'Not that well, but I know he was the Floor Manager for *Chartair's Challenge*.'

'Ah, this is getting interesting.' Stoker considered how much to tell Gaskill. 'It was the death of Mr Hansby that I was originally investigating when I heard about Mr Hamilton. I can confirm that he died a few days ago, in mysterious circumstances. He too had recently stepped up his security arrangements.'

Gaskill's face had turned white as a sheet. 'Oh my God! Then Max could be right!'

'Tell me what he said.'

'He said that there's a madman out there hell-bent on getting them; to kill all of them!' Gaskill buried his face in his hands. 'I don't think I can take this,' he moaned.

Stoker looked with some sympathy at the troubled man. 'I'm sorry to push you, but I need to know exactly what Mr Chartair said.'

'I . . . I ddd . . . don't know, I can't th . . . think. You'd better talk to him yourself.' Gaskill staggered to a nearby desk and pulled a notebook from a drawer. 'His number's in here. You can use my ttt . . . telephone.'

'Good idea.' Stoker went to the telephone, which rested on a table in the hallway. He dialled the number he had been given, waited for several rings and was about to hang up when the phone was answered.

'Hello?'

'Is that Mr Chartair?'

'Speaking.'

'Mr Chartair, my name is Vincent Stoker. I'm phoning from Mr Gaskill's apartment. I'm a private investigator and I've been retained to look into some recent deaths.'

There was a pause.

'Mr Chartair?'

'Sorry. I'm still here. So it's true then, Larry's been murdered.' It was a statement rather than a question. 'I guess I'm next.'

'What makes you say that?' Stoker asked.

'I suppose I'd better explain.'

The story that Chartair went on to tell Stoker over the next fifteen or so minutes was one he found hard to believe and yet, given the circumstances and the evidence he had at his disposal, equally hard to refute. Apparently, several weeks into shooting the latest series of *Chartair's Challenge* something strange had happened. A young man called Andrei Weizak had come on, purporting to possess telekinetic abilities, and had been given his opportunity to prove his claim in order to scoop the prize money. As specified by the rules of the show, he had been tested and the talents he had demonstrated had been truly amazing.

After having been searched to ensure that he had no concealed magnets or wires, Weizak repeatedly raised and lowered a series of miscellaneous objects by the power of his mind alone.

The reaction amongst the crew had been mixed, for whereas Conway had been deeply impressed but keen to test Weizak further, Chartair and Hansby had been dismissive and defensive. Chartair, in particular, admitted he had taken an instant dislike to the 'long-haired hippy' and had fully intended to make a mockery of his claims. When confronted with what, on the surface, looked an authentic demonstration of psychic ability, the presenter had immediately decided to set another challenge — demanding that Weizak use his telekinetic powers to levitate *him*.

To the surprise of all, Weizak had obliged.

Suspended in mid-air, ten feet off the ground, Chartair, screaming to be let down, had shouted curses at Weizak while Hansby and Conway stared in disbelief.

Weizak had set Chartair back on the

ground. Right hand extended, palm up and with a broad grin on his face, he had asked for the prize money.

It was at that point that a white-faced Hamilton had come down from the control room. Calling Hansby, Chartair and Conway into a hasty conference, he had asserted that on no account would they be paying out. There was, in fact, no fund set aside for it and he was damned if he was going to spend his own money on someone who, contrary to what Chartair now definitely believed, was nothing more than a low-down trickster. Ignoring protestations from Conway and Chartair that there was no explanation other than this being real, Hamilton started to make accusations, even going so far as to suggest that Chartair and Weizak were in cahoots and would split the prize money.

What happened then erased any lingering doubts as to the veracity of Weizak's claims. The door to the room had been torn off its hinges, revealing the furious figure of the 'contestant'. It was obvious that he had overheard their heated exchange and, clearly angered at the outcome, was now venting his wrath.

Chaos erupted.

Hamilton was thrown backwards by an invisible force and raised up the wall, his hands clasping at his throat. With nothing more than a stare, Weizak had upended the table and hurled it against Hansby. From outside the room there had come a crash as a lighting gantry fell to the floor and moments later the piercing trill of the fire alarm had sounded. It was at that point that Weizak had broken off his attack and opted to make an escape, leaving the burning studio. Everyone had got out but the show was shut down indefinitely, the crew paid off and the four principles left in a state of confusion and fear.

Stoker took a few moments to take in the tale that had poured out of Chartair. Trying to get his thoughts in order, he looked through the copious notes he had made. Finally, he cleared his throat. 'That's quite a story,' he said.

'I know what you're thinking, but I can assure you it's all true,' Chartair asserted.

'Well, it would certainly explain a lot if

it was but . . . can you be absolutely certain that this Weizak wasn't playing you somehow? Could he have had an accomplice among the crew?'

'Look, Mr Stoker, I've seen a hell of a lot of fraudsters on this show and I've worked in the entertainment business all my life. I know most of the smoke and mirrors tricks of the trade. Even if I didn't, Randall Conway does. He's an expert in magic, sleight of hand, illusion, everything you can think of, and he couldn't come up with a rational explanation for it. Larry was a fool not to pay out, even if he would have been out of pocket. If he had, he might be alive now.'

'You believe that Weizak is responsible for his death?'

'And James Hansby's. You heard about him I suppose?'

'Yes, but I'd be interested to know how *you* heard about his death. It's not supposed to be common knowledge.'

'I'm friendly with a couple of people he was working for, and news like that gets around.'

'Did many know about Weizak's outburst then? If the industry is so . . . interested in each other's business, could someone else be using Weizak as a fall guy? Someone who wanted to get rid of Hamilton and Hansby?'

'I doubt it. Larry could be annoying and he was hot-headed but there are plenty of others worse than him. And as for James Hansby, he was just doing his job. He wasn't influential enough to matter. Although, actually, it was Hansby who dealt with the rumours. He came up with the story that the show had been pranked by a special effects guy. Hamilton asked him to create a smoke screen to hide the truth. He wanted time to work out what to do.'

'That's what I don't really get, Mr Chartair. Surely if Mr Hamilton realised he had discovered someone with a truly amazing ability, he could have made far more money out of milking that than he would have paid out to Weizak? Why did he refuse?'

'To be honest, we were all in shock. Larry's never been great at thinking on his feet and he's a control freak to boot. I'm sure Randall and I could have talked him round if Weizak hadn't suddenly attacked us and ran off. I know Randall has tried to track the guy down, to talk to him off-camera. I've said that I can get him any deal he wants with the big networks.'

'This is a lot to get my head around.'

'Ha!' Chartair exclaimed. 'You think you've got problems! It looks like Weizak is intent on getting his revenge. At least, it might go in our favour that Randall and I tried to argue his case but I think the guy is a complete nut.'

'Have you talked to the police? Asked for protection?'

'I can just see that going down well! No, I'm going to lie low for a while, maybe see about getting a plane out of the country. It's obvious Weizak can get through any defences and I've had personal experience of his powers. I called Harvey to see if he can get a message through to Randall, to encourage him to do the same. With two of us dead, we can't take any chances. I don't think

Harvey believed just how serious this is. It sounds like Larry didn't tell him any of it, which, knowing Harvey's nervous disposition, makes a lot of sense.'

Stoker was thinking furiously. Whatever he himself believed, it was clear that Chartair was convinced he had to take evasive action. Dawson would want to interview the man and would be none too pleased to find him gone. 'Mr Chartair, the FBI are involved in this now. Would you be prepared to go with one of their agents to a safe house?'

'It's not a bad idea but I can't afford to wait around any longer. I've made up my mind. To hell with this! I'm leaving right now for the airport. If you give me a number to call, I'll be in touch once I'm safe but I'm not going to stay here a minute longer.'

'Okay.' Stoker read off the contact number for Dawson and Chartair noted it down. 'Just before you go, can you give me a description of this Andrei Weizak?'

'Slim, scrawny even, hair too long, clothes too tatty. Somewhere between a hippy and a bum. You could find half a dozen like him in LA if it weren't for his eyes . . . I'm never going to forget his eyes.'

5

Murder in Paradise

Under normal circumstances, Chartair's beachfront Malibu home would have been an idyllic paradise; a beautiful, exclusive, palm-fronded retreat from the hectic bustle of Los Angeles. It was a multi-million dollar property which rubbed shoulders with a veritable A-list of Hollywood celebrities and whilst its owner may not have been quite as high up the ladder himself, he had certainly accrued a large personal fortune to have been able to live in a place of such calibre.

Dawson's flight from San Francisco had been arranged at the last minute and Stoker had been waiting for him at the airport so they had wasted little time, even so, the forensic team and a considerable number of police officers were swarming over the house and grounds by the time they arrived.

Stoker introduced Dawson to Police Detective Lovenski who had just finished taking a lengthy statement from a young, smartly-dressed man with sandy brown hair.

'Pleased to meet you, detective,' said Dawson. 'Although I wish it could have been under better circumstances.' He shook Lovenski's hand. 'So, who was that you were talking to?'

'His name's Bud Williams. He was Chartair's chauffeur. Seems that Chartair had given instructions to his domestic staff to take time off for a few weeks but Williams had received a call to hurry over and take his employer to the airport.'

'And presumably it was Williams who reported the death?' Dawson asked.

The police detective nodded. 'That's right. When he arrived, he saw the . . . mess inside and followed the trail of blood round to the tennis court.'

'I take it that's where the body was found?' Stoker asked.

'Yeah, it's still there if you want to take a look. If you have the stomach for it. It's the weirdest thing I've ever seen,'

Lovenski admitted. 'Come on, follow me. I'll give you the tour.'

Dawson followed the other two into the house.

Lovenski pointed to the door which had been partially forced off its hinges. 'There's little doubt that this is how the intruder got in. It would then appear that he came along this corridor and into the main lounge.' He pushed open a door to reveal a scene of destruction. For what had once been a splendidly furnished room, filled with the trappings of wealth; a baby grand piano, an ultra-modern aquarium, sleek white sofas and a cabinet full of trophies, now looked as though a tornado had hit it.

Dawson's eyes were drawn to the blood smeared, man-shaped imprint in one wall.

A pair of wrecked French windows led out to the gardens, the swimming pool and the tennis court beyond.

A team of forensic experts were painstakingly recording whatever they could find; filling small bags with items of interest and dusting for fingerprints.

'From the evidence we've gathered it

would appear that the victim was violently flung against the wall and probably thrown elsewhere, judging from the various blood stains and broken items, before somehow making his way outside in a futile escape attempt,' Lovenski said. 'The best is yet to come. This way.' Following a trail of blood, he led the way out of the French windows and down a small flight of stone steps. 'We've left the body in place for you. Like I said before, it's not pretty.'

They approached the tennis court.

Over to one side, lying sprawled on the clay, was the terribly lacerated corpse of Chartair. He had been so tightly constricted, from ankles to neck, by the tennis net which was wrapped around him that the cords had bitten into his skin, crisscrossing his flesh — transforming parts of him into something resembling a bloody, padded quilt. His eyes were wide, his face was purple; veins corded at his neck and his tongue lolled from his open mouth. And yet, despite the disfiguration, the face was all too familiar — for it was a visage that many living in Southern California had probably spent more time looking at than their own, such had been the victim's level of fame and popularity.

'A nasty way to go, huh?' Lovenski commented. 'Feel free to vomit, most of us have.'

'It's hard to believe I was talking to him only yesterday.' Stoker looked grimly at the gory sight. 'He was all set to leave. I guess the poor bastard just wasn't quick enough.'

'That makes sense. There were two hastily packed suitcases in the hall. So, what actually do you know about this, Vince? You didn't say much on the phone.' Lovenski looked enquiringly between the two.

Dawson took the lead. 'Well, you know some of it already. We've reason to believe that someone has been mounting a targeted attack on several people involved with a particular programme. It was only yesterday that Mr Stoker narrowed it down to *Chartair's Challenge.*'

'*Chartair's Challenge?* Never heard of it. Saying that, I don't have time to watch much TV,' Lovenski admitted.

'That doesn't matter. Suffice to say that Mr Chartair was convinced that a disgruntled contestant, Andrei Weizak, was out to get him.' Dawson looked down at the fleshy remains. For some obscene reason it made him think of dead fish and octopi in a trawlerman's haul. 'I think we have to conclude he was right.'

'*Andrei Weizak?* Excellent. We'll put out an APB for him.' Lovenski reached for his police radio.

'I . . . think before you do that, we should fill you in on the rest of the story,' Dawson said. 'Is there somewhere quiet we can go?'

★   ★   ★

Dawson was becoming increasingly concerned about Stoker's driving. The private investigator had a devil-may-care attitude to the rules of the road. Then again, he too felt that time was of the essence. Reasoning that Randall Conway — the psychic debunker — was probably next on Weizak's hit list, the sooner they could get him into protective custody the better.

'I hope I'm going the right way,' Stoker said.

Silently, Dawson cursed the fact that they had been unable to reach Conway by telephone. At least he lived fairly near to Chartair. Other police were being scrambled to meet them but, certainly with the speed Stoker was going, they stood a good chance of getting there first.

Knuckles whitening as he clutched the steering wheel, Stoker threw the car into a sharp turn, narrowly avoided an oncoming coach, and sped along the road like a getaway driver, weaving in and out of yet more traffic.

Angry car horns blared.

'Do you really think this Weizak has telekinetic abilities?' Dawson asked. He was unsure as to the wisdom of interrupting Stoker's concentration but it was a question that needed asking for if that was the case then just how dangerous might an encounter with him prove to be?

'Could be. Hell, why not? There are plenty of people who believe in that kind of thing. Who's to say that they aren't right?' Stoker replied. 'Haven't you read *Carrie*?'

'Can't say that I have.'

'Well, that's all about a — ' With a screech of tyres, Stoker braked suddenly as a camper van filled with teenage kids ambled on to the coast road from a layby. The car slewed and came to a stop.

'Did you ever do the driver training course at the Bureau?' Dawson asked neutrally, when he had got his breath back.

'Yeah,' Stoker replied as he moved off again, a little more slowly. 'Passed it too with flying colours.'

'I wasn't complaining, just . . . checking.' Dawson looked at the map that he had been consulting. It was one of several that covered Los Angeles and the surrounding area. 'I think we must be close now.'

They drove in silence for a few more minutes. Then Dawson pointed to a road that sloped down towards the coast. 'I think that must be it.'

Stoker turned the car into the road and followed it to the point where it petered out into a dirt track. He parked up.

'Do you want to wait for back-up?' Dawson asked.

'No time for that,' Stoker replied, drawing his handgun from its holster. 'Come on.'

Hazy clouds had covered the sun and a fresh breeze blew straight off the Pacific Ocean as Dawson stepped out of the car and surveyed the stretch of sand and rock at the end of which he could see the surprisingly modest, isolated, single-storey beach house owned by Conway. The view the property commanded was stunning, even if the building itself was relatively unimpressive. It was a direct contrast to the opulent homes occupied by Hamilton and Chartair, which was to be expected for the psychic debunker was less famous and would certainly have been paid a smaller fee. Nevertheless, it was still an enviable home. Nearing the front door, he gained the distinct impression that the house was deserted and had not been lived in for several days, perhaps weeks. His suspicions were confirmed upon noticing the empty garage and when he peered through a small window by the front door, he saw a profusion of unopened mail on the floor. Moving to another window, he looked through into what was obviously the living room.

There were no lights on and there were no signs of life.

The only sound came from the gentle wash of the sea and the occasional call of a seabird.

Bearing in mind the grisly deaths of Hamilton, Chartair and Hansby, Dawson felt a certain sense of foreboding as he drew his Bureau-issued firearm and tried the door handle. Was victim number four inside? If so, it was possible that the murderer could be nearby. Hell, for all he knew maybe Conway was the killer. Perhaps he harboured a grudge against the other three and had worked in partnership with Weizak.

'At least there's nothing to indicate forced entry,' said Stoker.

To Dawson's surprise, the front door was unlocked and, pushing it open, he stepped over the numerous scattered letters and entered the hall. 'Mr. Conway? Are you here?'

There was no reply.

Handgun held tightly, Dawson nodded

to Stoker and they began to move cautiously through the house. Five minutes later, they had established that it was unoccupied and more importantly, there was no corpse. There were, however, abundant signs that Conway had left in a hurry. In the bedroom, drawers had been pulled out and articles of clothing lay strewn on the floor. The refrigerator and kitchen cupboards were almost bare.

The signs were that the owner had either fled in fear of his life, in which case he must have thought that he was a target, or else he was the perpetrator and feared discovery.

Returning to the living room, Dawson turned on the lights and looked around. It was a comfortable space with a superfluity of unusual objects, many of which he recognised as standard magic show props; the kind of things that could no doubt be picked up for a few dollars. Others were more unique and he had no idea of their use or provenance. Two of the walls were lined with bookcases which reflected Conway's field of expertise. At a glance, he could see that much of it consisted of works on parapsychology, particularly dealing with the fields of ESP, clairvoyance and telekinesis. However, there were also studies concerning the darker side of magic; demonology, necromancy, witchcraft and the occult.

Resting on a coffee table was a signed copy of Anton LaVey's *The Satanic Bible*.

Stoker picked it up, suppressing a chuckle.

'I take it you've got one like that at home?' Dawson commented wryly.

'You're forgetting, I'm a Luciferian, not a Satanist. There *is* a difference.' Stoker put the book back.

They continued to search through the room.

What Dawson found most interesting was the fact that there were gaps in the shelves, indicating that certain volumes had been removed, probably recently judging by the disturbed dust. Had the owner of the house taken these with him when he had departed in such a hurry? If so, why? He then turned his attention to the pile of mail in the hallway. Gathering it all up, he found a clear surface in the kitchen and began to systematically work his way through, throwing aside those that were clearly junk. What remained consisted of several utility bills, communications from Conway's bank, and a reminder for payment on an outstanding balance at a local garage and several more interesting handwritten pieces of correspondence. Some of the latter were fan mail, with one or two invitations to investigate alleged paranormal incidents and whereas this looked interesting and possibly merited following up, it did not strike him as being vitally important or in any way attached to the case.

Stoker was examining a cabinet filled with bizarre, shamanistic artefacts. He closed the glass door and turned to Dawson. 'For a professional sceptic, Conway sure was interested in weird stuff.'

'He obviously took his job seriously,' Dawson agreed. 'I don't think we're going to find anything else here. Let's check the garage.' It was as he was opening the front door that he caught sight of a corner of white paper protruding from beneath a rug in the hallway. Bending down, he pulled it free, finding that it was another envelope which he had previously missed. It was secured with red sealing wax which had been imprinted with a circular design that he did not recognise. Opening his penknife, he carefully slit the top edge of the envelope and removed the piece of paper inside.

Mr Conway
The more I think about what you told me, the more I am led to believe that you are right. Time works against us and I will prepare what I can here but as I know you are in possession of a copy of Tuska Grembi's Bardo Thodol I strongly advise you to bring it with you. This at least may give us a fighting chance.
H the P

Intrigued, Dawson checked the date of the postmark, noting that the letter had been sent only a couple of days ago. Certain that he had seen the work referred to amongst Conway's collection, he returned to the living room, scanned the shelves and retrieved the leather-bound tome. Like many of the others, it appeared to be a treatise on various aspects of spirituality and the occult; written in a language he had never seen before. There were numerous illustrations of mystical creatures and bizarre sigils, all of which meant absolutely nothing to him or to Stoker.

★　★　★

The Los Angeles-based Bureau researcher, Ted Kowalski, nodded as he handed the envelope back. He was a short, bespectacled, portly individual who had been just about to leave the office and head home for the evening when Dawson and Stoker had turned up. 'Absolutely no doubt about it; the seal is unmistakable. We've been keeping tabs on this lot for at least ten years.' He patted a file on the desk in front of him. 'It's all in here, not that there's very much.'

'So who are they?' Dawson asked.

'They're a cult,' Kowalski answered. 'They refer to themselves as the *Children of Haggai*. They started up in the mid-sixties as a hippy commune just south of San Diego, close to the Mexican border — the usual; free love and cannabis types. Flower power weirdos. Then, under their self-appointed leader, Derek Wilder, who calls himself Haggai the Prophet, they moved out to a remote hideout in the Mojave Desert some forty miles or so south of Vegas. That was when they started to get into some really bizarre stuff. Witchcraft and things. We have an account from one cult member who managed to break free.'

'What did he have to say?' said Dawson, interestedly. He had had dealings with cult activity in the past, notably the *Peoples Temple* and the *Crescent Mooners* — the latter being a band of what the Bureau called '*Apocaloonies*' who had firmly believed in both the impending end of the world and its subsequent annexation by a nine-foot lizard race from Saturn. Their activities had bordered on the unbelievable at times and they had been found guilty of numerous murders. Things had deteriorated further when the daughter of a well-respected senator had become indoctrinated and the authorities had decided that a full-scale assault on the compound was justified. Unfortunately, many of the cultists had committed suicide rather than allow themselves to be apprehended. He could only hope that these *Children of Haggai* would not be as extreme.

'Well, not a lot really. The usual stuff — a rigid timetable of teaching, mostly the Old Testament, strict vegetarian diet, no alcohol but a high intake of recreational drugs. The account given of Wilder was of a deluded, charismatic megalomaniac and yet one who, believe it or not, was allegedly in possession of some sort of magical powers.' Kowalski snorted derisively.

'*Magical . . . powers?*' Stoker deadpanned. 'What, like pulling a rabbit out of a hat?'

'Not quite.' Kowalski removed his spectacles and gave them a quick clean before putting them back on. 'Now, the thing to remember is this is coming from what I would class as a traumatised individual. I don't think we're talking about your usual desert dwelling, snake-handling religious freak. He claims that he witnessed things that defy explanation. Psychokinesis, conjuring fires, speaking with the dead.'

'Could this possibly have happened under the influence of narcotics?' Stoker asked, a smile hovering about his lips.

Kowalski nodded. 'I wouldn't be at all surprised, but Wilder has a very interest-ing history. Our files on *him* go back a long way.'

'Okay, tell me more,' said Dawson.

Kowalski selected one of his folders and opened it to the first page. 'Here's a fairly recent mugshot.'

Dawson was not sure what he had been expecting but the face that stared out at him, whilst not resembling Charles Manson, was certainly arresting. It was that of a somehow ageless bald man with a high, unwrinkled forehead, pronounced cheekbones, large, dark, almond-shaped eyes, a thin line of a mouth and little more than black slits for nostrils. In essence, he strongly resembled a human version of the archetypal Roswell Grey. Indeed, there was a certain alien quality about him and it would be easy to imagine someone like him possessing mesmeric powers and being able to command others to do his will; to think as he wanted them to think.

'He looks like something out of *Star Trek*,' Stoker commented.

'Yep, one weird looking guy,' Kowalski said. His telephone rang and he offered the file to Dawson to take a look at.

Carrying the papers to a nearby desk, Dawson flicked through the information. His investigative expertise coming to the fore, he quickly absorbed the facts. Believed to have been born in 1913, Wilder had served in a Canadian regiment during the Second World War. Returning to the United States, he had embarked on a life of petty crime before developing an unhealthy interest in science fiction and the supernatural. He claimed that he had seen flying saucers over Western Germany whilst on the push to Berlin and had conversed with otherworldly beings. It transpired that his mother, who had purported to be of Russian extraction — and had herself been 'of interest' to the authorities — held similar beliefs, combining her 'blood and thunder' biblical preaching with extreme superstitions. Following her death in 1960, he travelled extensively in the Far East — China, Nepal and Tibet — before coming back and embarking on a three year road trip traversing the West Coast gathering a cabal of like-minded individuals.

His telephone call finished, Kowalski came over. 'So, why do you want to know about Wilder and the *Children of Haggai*?'

'I think there might be a connection between them and a series of unusual deaths I've been investigating.' Dawson looked up from the papers. 'Hamilton, Chartair and Hansby. Have you heard about them?'

'You're on *that* case?' Kowalski asked, his eyes lively. 'I've heard bits and pieces, certainly.'

'I'm almost sure they're murders committed by the same person, or persons, and I've got a suspicion that whoever sent that letter, presumably Wilder, knows something about it.' Dawson took a sip of water from a plastic cup. 'I definitely need to check it out. Is this cult under active surveillance at the moment?'

'No.' Kowalski shook his head. 'As far as we're aware, no crimes other than substance abuse are being committed at this time. Our informant was debriefed when he left them as part of general intelligence gathering. It's not a crime to be weird, especially not here in California. Hell, if it were half the population would be behind bars.' He regarded Dawson and Stoker as if weighing them up. 'I'd be careful if you go out there though. Can you take a team along?'

'I'll bear it in mind. Still, I should ask for clearance, judging from your file. I'm not about to storm the place. My main intention is to talk to someone who may have visited them, may still be there. He's not a weirdo.' Dawson paused remembering the numerous books on the occult at Conway's house. 'Probably not, anyway.'

'Well, good luck. Their location is here somewhere,' Kowalski said, flipping through the file until he found the relevant page.

'Thanks. I'll tell you what the place is like when I get back.'

'Just make sure you *do* get back,' Kowalski said, only half-jokingly.

6

Terror in Tinseltown

Even though it was mid-morning, it was already baking hot on Hollywood Boulevard. Crowds of tourists moved along the sidewalk, stopping frequently to take photographs or to purchase cheap souvenirs from the numerous shops along the way.

'I must confess, I've never actually been along here before. Driven by it, yes, but not actually stopped to take a look,' Stoker said, staring down, with some interest, at the brass star inserted into the sidewalk of the Hollywood Walk of Fame.

'Me neither,' Dawson replied. 'Do you know if Chartair had one of these?'

'No idea. Although, if he didn't, he might get one posthumously,' Stoker reasoned. He had collected Dawson from the modest motel he had spent the night at in time for breakfast and to work out how they would deal with their potential new informant. The single piece of paper in Kowalski's file on Wilder that listed known or suspected contacts had caught his attention the moment he spotted a name he particularly recognised — Samantha De'Carlo. Seeing as Burt Lancaster, Mickey Rooney and Elvis Presley were also on the list, he did not lend it much credence but it was still worth following up. A telephone call to her home had set up this morning's meeting in a bar near to where she was due to film a few scenes for a television special.

Rounding a corner, they saw up ahead a large line of people queuing to get into a cinema to see a morning screening of one of the year's blockbuster movies — *The Omen*, starring Gregory Peck and Lee Remick.

'I take it you've seen that one already?' Dawson asked.

'Yeah, it's not bad.' Stoker thought for a moment. 'There are one or two weird death scenes in it not unlike what we're investigating.' He lit up a cigarette and took a deep drag. 'The bar should be just up ahead. It's supposed to be near the

Brown Derby.' Leading the way, he waited for a gap in the traffic before crossing the busy road and turning down Vine Street. A little further on, he saw the iconic Spanish Mission style building and, just beyond, a much smaller venue called *Roxette's*.

They entered the stylish foyer and approached the bar.

It was busy inside with a wide variety of clientele. People were laughing, joking, eating a late breakfast or enjoying a pre-lunch cocktail. The sweet smell of maple syrup, waffles, cream-covered cookies and cigarette smoke filled the air.

Stoker spotted De'Carlo and Wolf after a few moments and went over to their table in the corner.

'Hello, Vincent. Nice to see you again.' De'Carlo smiled winningly and gestured for Stoker and Dawson to sit down. 'And you must be Special Agent Dawson? I'm honoured.'

The slightly teasing intonation almost made Dawson blush. 'I'm pleased to meet you Miss De'Carlo and Mr . . . ?' He looked questioningly at her grizzled companion.

'Just call me Wolf,' the older man in the leather jacket replied guardedly.

Stoker was about to say something when a waitress came over. He hastily ordered two coffees and declined any food. When she had gone, he stubbed out his cigarette and turned to De'Carlo. 'It's good to see that the threats you've been getting aren't keeping you from living your life as normal.'

'There's no way I'd let anyone stop me. I've got a sweet deal on a TV series that we're doing some preliminary filming for today,' De'Carlo answered. 'Fred Doyle Junior, who just so happens to be one of the biggest names here in Hollywood, has personally chosen me to feature in the opening scene of one of his programmes and there's no way I'd miss out on an opportunity like that. Besides, I feel perfectly safe with Wolf. I mean, would you go up against him?'

Dawson looked closely at Wolf and privately decided that he was probably capable enough in a fight, if a little old. He also noticed the gun butt that protruded slightly from beneath the bearded man's jacket.

'I appreciate that you've got a busy schedule so let's get straight to the point,' Stoker said. 'I need to ask you something. Does the name Derek Wilder mean anything to you?'

The effect was immediate. De'Carlo's eyes widened and she broke into a laugh. '*Derek Wilder*? Of course I've heard of him. What do you want to know about that charlatan?'

'Whatever you can tell us,' said Dawson.

'Okay. It must have been five, maybe six years ago. I was introduced to him at a party. I think it might have been Vincent Price's sixtieth birthday. Wilder had come along with someone or other and was networking big time; toadying up to people left, right and centre. He was going on and on about this religious thing he was setting up. Half-pseudo-science, half-mysticism. All bullshit.' De'Carlo gave a derisory shake of her head.

'What's he like?' Dawson asked curiously.

'Physically . . . kind of weird-looking.

130

Thin and with really tight, dry skin, almost like a reptile. Definitely creepy, but he has a hell of a way with words. While you're talking to him, his kooky stuff sounds almost believable. I've no doubt he was trying to recruit that night and he called me a couple of times after.' De'Carlo took a sip from her iced tea. 'I think he was targeting people with money; financial backers more than followers as such. I think he had plenty of those but they were the lost and the lonely, rather than the idle rich. I heard later that he'd adopted some kind of biblical name and had taken a load of people off to the desert in order to enlighten them or something like that. Maybe he thinks he's Moses leading the Hebrew slaves out of Egypt to the Promised Land.' She laughed. 'I dare say he's living under a rock somewhere along with the other lizards.'

'You called him a charlatan. Care to expand on that?' Dawson asked.

'Well, I remember he made these outrageous claims. The usual nonsense. He said that he could teach us to perform miracles; that he had powers he was willing to share . . . for a 'small' donation.' De'Carlo smiled mockingly. 'Just *how* small he never got round to saying.'

'Can you remember anything he specifically claimed he could do?' Stoker said.

De'Carlo thought for a moment. 'To be honest, I can't really remember. It's a while ago and in my profession I meet a lot of weirdos. Present company excepted of course.'

'And have you heard anything of him since?' Stoker enquired.

De'Carlo shook her head. 'Sorry, not for years.'

'Well, I have,' Wolf butted in, his deep voice almost a growl. 'After Samantha gave him the brush off, he tried to contact her several times but Maureen and I told him where to get off. The guy's a loony. Persistent, I'll give him that, but still a loony.'

'The dangerous kind?' Stoker asked.

'I wouldn't think so. More deluded than anything else.' With a gnarled hand, Wolf scratched at his beard. 'Why are you interested in Wilder anyway? Do you think he has something to do with these death threats?'

'There's nothing to indicate that he is but he could be peripherally involved in another case I'm working on and when I saw there was a link with Miss De'Carlo I wanted to follow it up. Which leads me to another question. It's a bit of a long shot, but have you by any chance ever heard of a man called Andrei Weizak?' Stoker said. He thanked the waitress for his coffee and set it down, accidentally spilling a sizeable amount over Dawson's white shirt cuff and earning a disgruntled look which he ignored entirely.

'No, can't say as I have,' De'Carlo said. 'Certainly doesn't sound familiar. Who is he and where does he fit into this?'

'It's a long story,' Dawson answered, dabbing at the coffee stain with a napkin. 'However, I believe you heard about the death of Larry Hamilton. Well, it could be that he's involved.'

'Oh?' De'Carlo was interested.

'We're trying to establish a link at the moment and, unfortunately, I can't go into any more detail.' Dawson looked around for the restroom.

Wolf glanced at his watch. 'Samantha, it's later than I thought. We'd better not keep Mr Doyle waiting.'

Dawson excused himself and, having spotted the restroom, headed in that direction in order to remove the offending coffee stain.

'I guess that's my cue to get going,' De'Carlo said as she picked up her handbag and got to her feet. 'I hope our brief conversation's been of some help.'

'Thanks again. I'll be in touch soon,' Stoker said.

Leaving a generous tip, De'Carlo and Wolf made their way to the exit.

Stoker finished his coffee and thought things over. Was it stretching coincidence too far to think Wilder was in some way complicit in the deaths that they were laying at Weizak's door? The only connection so far was the rather cryptic letter from Wilder to Conway, but that could have been about anything. His gut feeling was that there *would* turn out to be a link but they did not have enough information yet. It was just a question of finding all the pieces of the jigsaw and then trying to put them together in order to solve the puzzle.

The waitress returned in order to collect the money.

Stoker was jolted from his thoughts by the noisy screech of brakes outside the restaurant.

There then came the unmistakable sound of semi-automatic gunfire.

'*What the . . . ?*' With a curse, Stoker sprang from his chair, drew his automatic, clicked off the safety catch and, forcibly pushing aside a fat, curious diner, dashed for the entrance. Ten feet away, Wolf lay sprawled face down on the sidewalk in a pool of blood. Looking to his right, he saw De'Carlo being dragged, kicking and screaming, by two armed men. One wore a rubber Gerald Ford mask, the other was disguised as Richard Nixon. They were trying to force her into the back of a black van.

'*Help me!*' De'Carlo screamed.

'Lyndon Johnson', who was sat in the driver's seat, noticed the private investigator, raised his Uzi submachine gun and opened fire, smashing windows and peppering stonework as Stoker leapt for cover.

Chaos and confusion erupted on the street.

There was more screaming as people fled. Others stared in amazement, perhaps wondering, given the locale, if this was an action sequence for an attraction or a movie being acted out for their entertainment. Similar things happened quite frequently.

A further burst of deafening gunfire sprayed the doorway to *Roxette's*.

Their hostage secure, 'Ford' and 'Nixon' clambered inside, yelling at the driver to make good their escape. Throwing his Uzi onto the passenger seat, 'Johnson' stepped on the gas.

Stoker emerged from the bullet-riddled doorway. The van's rear door was still open and, as the vehicle passed, he raised his automatic, took aim and blasted two hollow-pointed slugs into 'Ford'.

The dead man tumbled from the rear door.

Oblivious to the danger and the

screams from the throngs of onlookers, Stoker sprinted down the middle of the street in pursuit. Oncoming cars, motorbikes and a bus packed with tourists flashed past like blurs, his sight and mind focused solely on the black van which was now getting further away. He saw the getaway vehicle jump the lights at an intersection before taking a tight right corner. Chasing after it, lungs burning, sweat beading on his forehead in the intense heat, he knew that his chances of catching up were dwindling fast and what that meant for De'Carlo was not even worth thinking about. With that thought, a flash of hatred ignited within him, temporarily dispelling the pain he was now feeling in his legs. Gun grasped firmly, he ran on, reaching the corner just in time to see his quarry disappear down another street some two hundred yards away.

There were a couple of fatalities lying on the ground, unfortunate pedestrians who had been indiscriminately and callously mown down.

Stoker heard more gunfire and was

then surprised to see the black van reverse, at speed, back into the main street, perhaps to avoid becoming snarled in traffic. Vaulting agilely over the hood of a taxi which had screeched to a braking halt in front of him, and ignoring the angry protests from its Oriental occupant, he sped off down the street. Everything was becoming surreal in the manner that events far out of the ordinary have a tendency to do and it was only his rigorous physical and mental discipline, coupled with his previous training in the Bureau that enabled him to keep a firm hold on the reality of the situation.

Distant police sirens warbled.

Car horns blared.

Too many late nights, too many stiff drinks, too many greasy takeaways and too many cigarettes were now beginning to have their effect on the private investigator. Breathing heavily, he wiped the sweat from his eyes and was momentarily stunned to see the black van now weaving its way through the traffic towards him, its driver having been unable to take any other route. 'Nixon' had now crammed himself into the passenger seat and was leaning out of the window, opening fire with his Uzi on anything that got in their way in an attempt to clear their path.

A withering burst of gunfire cut down two LAPD officers as they rushed, firearms at the ready, from a burger joint.

Grimly, Stoker stood his ground. Automatic held tightly in both hands, he took aim as the van veered across the street. Squeezing on the trigger, he fired three times in the manner he had been instructed to do at the Bureau's training academy — feet apart, arms extended, gun raised to eye level, wrists taking the strain from the powerful recoil.

All three slugs struck 'Nixon' — the gunman's head exploding in a bloody mess. His Uzi fell from lifeless hands onto the ground.

The police sirens were getting louder. Much louder.

Stoker could clearly see 'Johnson' through the van's windscreen as the driver shifted gears and accelerated, heading straight for him. For a split second, he considered taking a shot but hurriedly decided to leap clear, the speeding vehicle missing him by a matter of inches. With a mad scramble, he reached out for the rear door which was swinging open, missed it and ended up stumbling into the path of an oncoming cop car. The bright, red glare of its flashing light stabbed at his eyes as, tyres smoking, it mercifully drew to a halt just in front of him. Racing round it, he chased after the departing vehicle.

More traffic spilled out from various intersections.

Briefly, Stoker saw De'Carlo in the back of the van moments before it went into a wide skid. It then smashed into a white stretched limousine which sent the luxury sedan careering onto the sidewalk.

A tinted passenger window lowered and a shocked Hollywood actor, champagne bottle in hand and glamorous, scantily-clad 'lady friend' at his side, stared out.

'This is the LAPD! Put down your weapon!' an almost mechanical voice shouted from a loudhailer.

Paying the police warning no heed,

Stoker continued to race after the black van which was now leaving a trail of carnage as it recklessly battered its way through the traffic, forcing other vehicles off the street. The sound of car horns raged in his ears, adding to the madness. And then, to his shock, he heard the *pop-pop* of gunshots behind him and realised that the cops were actually trying to take *him* down. Bullets whizzed past. 'Holy shit!' he cursed.

Nearby, an unfortunate motorcyclist lay half-in, half-out of the large, smashed window of an amusement arcade.

The biker's vehicle looked relatively undamaged and, throwing his automatic aside, Stoker hauled it upright, jumped on, revved the engine and sped off. It had been several years since he had last been in the saddle but it was amazing how quickly it all came back to him. He felt the motorbike lunge forward like an unchained animal, full of power and strength. The wheels hummed on the road. Weaving in and out of the traffic, he began to gain ground on the van. He hunched slightly forward, a tense expression on his face, gritting his teeth, mouth twisted into a faint sneer. High-rise buildings, with large advertising billboards, flashed past as the speedometer hit fifty, then fifty-five miles per hour. He was getting close. Very close. This was when he had to hope that an Uzi-wielding 'JFK' was not in there along with De'Carlo. Now that he was a clear target, one quick burst of machine gun-fire and it would all be over.

The van tore out onto the Hollywood Freeway — a chaotic, perpetually busy, frequently congested, multiple-laned, driver's nightmare.

'Welcome to Hell' was the sign that should have indicated the approach, for Stoker was well aware that the traffic here was crazy at the best of times. Add to that the infernal heat and the noisome stench of exhaust fumes and it was little surprise that he regarded this road system as one of the worst places on the planet — it was certainly one of the most dangerous. There was hardly a day went by without news coverage of a major accident, a police chase or a gang-related gun battle. He heard the sirens and then, in his left-hand wing-mirror, he saw, some distance behind, three cop cars tearing up the road in pursuit. His hands clenched tightly on the motorbike's handlebars, white-knuckled with the nervous pressure he was exerting.

Everywhere, harsh, blinding sunlight glinted off glass and chrome.

There was a deafening crescendo of blaring car horns.

Without warning, an eighteen wheel gasoline truck, doing somewhere in the region of eighty-five miles per hour, thundered past Stoker, its driver either drunk, asleep or suicidal. It rammed into the side of the black van, almost bowled it over like a skittle, then went into a violent jack knife before his very eyes. Perhaps due to the possibility of his own death, it was moments like this that made him feel truly alive. Lucifer Himself must have been looking out for the private investigator that day, for, by some miracle, he managed to swing the motorbike out of harm's way and narrowly avoided the tipping tanker full of flammable liquid.

Sparks flew as the huge, metallic,

cylindrical vessel scraped along the freeway.

Knowing full well what was going to happen, Stoker twisted the throttle and zoomed away.

The explosion that followed was cataclysmic as with an ear-splitting, brain-numbing bang, a ferocious wave of fire blasted out in all directions. Twisted wreckage flew everywhere. A burning tyre bounced off the roof of a yellow school bus packed with young kids on the other side of the freeway.

Ears ringing from the thunderous explosion, his body jarred and shaken by the blast, Stoker managed to retain control of the motorbike even as bits of debris began to fall all about him. He felt the searing heat at his back and, with a quick look over his right shoulder, saw the rising column of dense, black smoke. There was an acrid stench in his nostrils. Behind him, he could hear the terrible sounds of cars colliding; bonnets crumpling, horns blaring, tyres braking, glass shattering. Leaving the destruction in his wake, he revved the motorbike for all it was worth and sped after the black van which had switched lanes and was now heading for a looped flyover turning off the freeway.

Over to the right, the towering sky-scrapers of Los Angeles rose high, the skyline seeming to shimmer in the sweltering heat.

Suddenly, one of the black van's rear tyres blew. Rubber flapping noisily, the vehicle rebounded off a road barrier, slewed into the middle lane and crashed violently into the back of a delivery van.

The motorbike's speedometer, which had been reading close to sixty miles per hour, now began to slip back, the red needle falling to fifty and then forty. Knowing this was his best chance, Stoker rode up to the scene of the accident. Jumping off the motorbike, the private investigator approached the black van, stunned and elated to see De'Carlo clamber free. She was dazed and shaken up, with a nasty-looking cut above her left eye. That aside, she was in remarkable shape considering the ordeal she had just survived. Rushing forward, he put an arm around her, supporting her and leading her away.

People were getting out of their cars.

'Let me help. I'm a paramedic,' a tall, bearded man said as he approached.

From the sounds of it, cop cars and other emergency vehicles were closing in from every direction.

'Say, isn't that Lucretia Mortis?' Chewing gum, a plump-faced teenager stared in awe at his idol. 'I want her autograph.'

Before Stoker could respond, 'Johnson' staggered into view, his shirt and the mask he wore bloody from where he had obviously been injured. In his right hand, he held an Uzi. Obviously deciding his best option was to flee, rather than go out in a blaze of glory; he turned, awkwardly clambered over a low concrete wall and made a loping dash for it.

'Look after her.' Stoker left De'Carlo in the capable hands of the paramedic and went in pursuit of the gunman. Unarmed, he knew it was a foolhardy thing to do but there was a part of him that, ever since his family had been killed, no longer cared about his own safety. Dropping to the other side of the low wall, he noticed the discarded ex-president mask and saw his target, less than fifty yards away, heading towards a long-abandoned junk-yard.

And then the would-be kidnapper was frantically scaling a ten foot high, chain-linked fence, falling onto hands and knees on the other side. Within moments, he was up and out of sight, disappearing into the veritable labyrinth of rusted mounds formed from teetering piles of tyres and wrecked vehicles.

The fence rattled as Stoker went over it. Eyes darting from side to side, he cautiously yet quickly walked forward.

Spots of blood on the dusty ground formed a trail which led off to the right.

Following it, Stoker made his way through the junkyard, well aware that each breath he took could be his last. Reaching a three way intersection amongst the artificial mountains of twisted metal, he came to an abrupt halt. Inwardly, he felt tense, every muscle and fibre of his body taut and tight. Crouching down, he picked up a four foot long piece of steel piping, pleased to feel its solidity in his hand. It was a poor weapon when compared to a sub-machinegun but it was undeniably better than nothing.

There was the sound of approaching sirens.

Stoker hoped that he would get to 'Johnson' before the cops did. Peering through a gap between two precariously balanced burnt out cars, he saw him, just a matter of yards away. Breathing painfully, the man was leaning against a rusty oil drum upon which his Uzi rested. A not insubstantial pool of blood had gathered around his feet and, as the private investigator watched, he saw the wounded man remove a six-inch long shard of glass from his right leg.

An LAPD helicopter had been dispatched and was now in the air, circling overhead.

Stealthily, like a panther stalking its prey, Stoker sneaked up. Then, having reached striking distance, he raised the length of steel before bringing it down with a powerful, two-handed swing.

Metal struck flesh with a sickening crunch.

'Johnson' went flying.

Stoker advanced and swung out a second time, cracking a vicious blow across his victim's upper torso. Like Babe Ruth waiting for the pitch, he paused for a moment, then violently struck again — breaking an arm.

'Johnson' lay badly battered on the ground; a wiry, thirty-something year old with tattooed arms, missing front teeth and a mop of corn-yellow curly hair — a hoodlum of the lowest breed. A hired thug; there must have been thousands like him in Los Angeles doing dirty work for their Underworld masters. He was twitching spasmodically and his eyes were wide and tinged red; clear indicators that he was high on something.

'Who are you?' Stoker demanded. Without waiting for an answer, he kicked the fallen man full in the guts. 'Why were you after De'Carlo? Tell me, punk, or I'll finish you here and now!'

'I . . . I've got rights. You can't — '

Not averse to meting out his own form

of justice, Stoker brought the metal pipe down twice more, shattering a kneecap and ensuring that this particular lowlife would never walk unaided again. '*Tell me!*'

Groaning loudly, 'Johnson' rolled onto his back. '*Aaaagh!* Okay, okay. We were sent by Maurice Goldberg.'

Stoker paused in surprise. Goldberg was a well-known television evangelist with a following of thousands.

'Drop the weapon or I'll fire!' a voice shouted.

Turning, Stoker saw an armed police officer thirty yards away. A second, and then a third joined their colleague.

More cops were soon swarming in from all sides.

Stoker let the length of pipe fall from his grip. Calmly, he raised his hands, placed them on his head and took several backward steps. Moments later, he was roughly handcuffed, searched and then bundled into the back of a police car.

7

On Film

Stoker had found the past thirty hours more exhausting than the high-speed chase. It had been an endless case of answering questions, giving statements and eating junk food at the LAPD headquarters as the explanation of the previous day's events gradually came to light. The District Attorney's sister-in-law had been one of those wounded in the incident and he was after blood. Along with the City Mayor, he was keen to pull out all the stops in order to get the private investigator prosecuted. Finally, however, the charges had been put on hold and he had been released pending further investigations. He and Dawson had agreed to meet back at his office at six o'clock that evening.

'Fourteen dead. Fifty-three injured — nineteen seriously.' Dawson sighed.

'You know, you're damned lucky that Lovenski's supporting you on this.'

'Unfortunate collateral damage.' Stoker reached into a drawer for his cigarettes. He lit up and inhaled deeply, taking the smoke deep into his lungs. 'The whole abduction attempt was a disaster. The three guys involved were all known to the police for various violent crimes. It's been established that the hostage-takers had injured several pedestrians even before I got involved. The one that survived was out of his head on coke. Once in the cells, he spilled everything on Goldberg. *That's* the lucky bit, *not* Lovenski's support, although I do appreciate it. The LAPD are far more interested in what they discovered at Goldberg's home. When it became clear that he was intending to burn Samantha alive, and film the whole thing, that became the focus of attention. I swung by her house once the cops let me go just to see how she was.'

'How's she doing?'

'Fine. A bit shaken up but otherwise okay. According to the hospital, it looks like Wolf's going to pull through which doesn't surprise me. He's a tough bastard. Samantha told me that he's ex-Marine Corps. Single-handedly took out a platoon of Japs at Iwo Jima . . . or so she said.'

'Glad to hear it,' Dawson replied. It had been a stressful ten minutes for him as he had administered first-aid to the wounded man before the ambulance arrived. He flicked once more through the *Bardo Thodol* that he had taken from Conway's house. From what little research he had done, he had established that the book was more commonly referred to as *The Tibetan Book of the Dead* — a corpus of mystical near-death visions and spiritual teachings — and that the author of this version, Tuska Grembi, had been a fourteenth century Tibetan nomad-monk. 'McMasters has allowed me some time to work on Chartair's murder so let's concentrate on Weizak.'

'Okay then, what's the latest on him?'

'Very little actually,' Dawson answered. 'He appears on police files over several years as a petty criminal, pulled in for car-jacking, shop-lifting and one case of attempted burglary. He's a drifter. No convictions for any violent crimes. No next of kin and hardly anything known about his background. Most importantly — current whereabouts unknown. There are mugshots of him and I've got those circulating. We might get lucky.'

'You know what would be useful — footage of his performance on *Chartair's Challenge*. That is, of course, if any survived the fire. Just to see if there is any truth in his so-called abilities. It'd certainly make interesting viewing.'

'Why didn't I think of that? Of course!' Dawson thought for a moment. 'Could be that Hamilton's secretary, Gaskill, might be able to help us. I'll call him.' He located the telephone number and, over the course of the next few minutes, explained his request to Gaskill.

'Hmm,' said Gaskill. 'I'll ask around but I know the damage to the building was pretty extensive. Larry told me they'd been hit by an electrical fire and that was why they'd stopped filming. That could have melted all of the film but you might be lucky. From what you told me Max had said, if there was any good footage then I'd bet good money that Buzz Hoskins would be holding on to it. He was the chief cameraman. I've got his details if you want them.'

Dawson took down the address and telephone number, thanked Gaskill and rang off.

'Any luck?' Stoker asked.

'Perhaps.' Dawson immediately picked up the telephone again and dialled Hoskins' number. The phone rang and rang but no one answered. With a curse, he looked once more at the address. 'Thirty-Sixth Street. Any idea where that is?'

'Yeah. It's over on the west side. A bit of a rough area but not too bad. We could get there in less than twenty minutes,' Stoker said. 'I can't think of anything better to do right now. Can you?'

In answer, Dawson picked up his jacket and the two left the office.

★   ★   ★

Stoker was right. Hoskins' neighbour-hood was not the best Los Angeles had to

155

offer but Dawson had seen worse. The cameraman's small, single-storey house was certainly in need of some repair; its picket fence looked like someone had inadvertently backed into it a few years ago and the grass had grown over the fallen posts. The front gate lay off its hinges and a rust-bucket of a car sat in the driveway.

'I don't think Hamilton paid too well, do you?' Stoker commented wryly. 'You would've thought that a professional cameraman could do better than this.'

Dawson shrugged. 'Some folk just aren't materialistic. I've got an uncle in New York who's worth millions but he chooses to live in a one-bedroom apartment in the Bronx.'

'*Why?* If I had that kind of money I'd be living it up in Vegas. Or maybe I'd buy a house in Hawaii.'

'He says it suits him. I don't know. Maybe he likes the rats and the cockroaches. He's always been a little strange.'

'It could be that Hoskins drinks all his pay away,' Stoker said, more cynically. Reaching the front door, he rapped on the frosted glass panel and then jumped back in alarm as a black shape threw itself at the door, barking furiously. 'Shit!'

'Take it easy,' Dawson said. Noticing that the private investigator's first instinct was to reach for his gun, he waved a calming hand and stepped forward himself. 'Mr Hoskins? Are you in?'

The dog continued to bark.

'Who's there?' a voice shouted from inside. 'I've got a double-barrel here and I'm not afraid to use it!'

'FBI, Mr Hoskins. I can show you my identification' said Dawson calmly. 'We'd like to ask you some questions about the work you did on *Chartair's Challenge*.'

The dog stopped barking for a moment and there came a low moaning sound.

Dawson and Stoker exchanged glances.

'Oh Jesus! I was right then, wasn't I? There *is* something damn weird going on.' Hoskins sounded defeated. 'Okay, give me a minute.'

There were shuffling and scratching sounds and then several bolts were drawn back and the door opened.

The figure that emerged was shockingly

dishevelled. Not a very old man, early sixties at the most but his eyes were bloodshot. A ragged, unkempt beard covered most of his face and his hair hung lankly. From the looks and smell of it his diet for the past week or so had been alcohol-heavy. 'I've shut Lassie out the back so that you can come in.'

'*Lassie?*' Stoker said, eyeing the muscled, black hound that was staring intently at them from a glass door leading to the yard. A low growl came from its saliva-flecked mouth.

'Yeah. She's very intelligent,' Hoskins said, unaware of the incongruity. 'You're welcome to sit down, if you can find a chair.'

'Thank you, Mr Hoskins.' Dawson shifted a pile of clothes from a wooden chair and sat. 'I take it, from the shotgun, that you're expecting trouble?'

Hoskins nodded. 'You can never be too careful. Lot of strange things happening of late. Things I can't get my head around. I guess that's why you're here, yeah?'

'What kind of things?' Stoker asked.

'That bloody freak, Weizak. He's on the

158

loose, isn't he?' The fear in Hoskins' voice was blatant.

'You might be right. What can you tell me about him?' Dawson asked.

'I don't think he's human. He can't be.' Hoskins spoke bluntly. 'The others didn't see the film. Even Larry Hamilton hasn't seen it. He refused to take a look. But I've seen it. I know that Weizak brought something with him.'

'What do you mean?' Dawson encouraged the cameraman.

'I . . . I can't tell you.' Hoskins shook his head, tiredly. 'You'd never believe me. But I can show you.' Following a nod of agreement from his two visitors, he led them into a small, dingy room at the back of the house. There were thick black curtains at the windows, and a screen had been set up on the rear wall. A projector and a threadbare sofa took up most of the space.

Dawson and Stoker took one look at the stained, dog hair-covered sofa and remained standing.

Hoskins shut the door behind them and switched the projector on. 'This is the

159

last piece of footage we captured and the only reel that survived the fire. I got it processed, even though it was badly damaged in places but . . . well, you'll see for yourselves. Watch closely. By the way, there's no audio.' Turning the light off, he started the film.

In the darkness, Dawson waited with some sense of unease, uncertain as to what he was about to see.

For a moment, there was nothing, then a grainy image appeared on the screen — a scratchy, black and white countdown from three to one. Then the film switched into colour, revealing a television studio with a psychedelically decorated backdrop. Standing in front of the swirling design were three people — Randall Conway, Max Chartair and a scruffy young man who had to be Andrei Weizak, dressed in grubby, threadbare jeans and a faded denim shirt.

Dawson took a step closer to the screen, scrutinising Weizak — his unkempt appearance fitted the description Stoker had given him.

Chartair was clearly talking to the

camera, his beaming smile carrying a discernible level of barely-concealed scepticism, inviting the viewer to share his unspoken derision. Then he stepped away and Randall Conway seemed to be interviewing Weizak.

'I'm going to skip forward a bit,' Hoskins said. 'This part's all just talking. From what I remember, Randall was asking the guy about what he claimed he could do. You can't see Max, he was out of shot, but he was smirking.' He wound the film on a little and restarted it. 'Here's where it gets interesting.'

Now the screen showed a wider shot, encompassing Weizak, Conway and a small table with various objects on it.

Dawson watched intently as a pocket watch slid across the table of its own accord. It was followed by a glass of water and a telephone directory, the latter falling off the edge. From the look on Conway's face he appeared interested but only mildly impressed. He said something to Weizak.

'That was Randall asking if the weirdo could move the actual table. Believe me;

161

it's heavier than it looks. Took two of us to carry,' Hoskins explained. 'We've caught a few quacks out that way.'

On screen, Weizak held his arms out, fingers spread. The table lurched, as though hauled by invisible wires, tipping off the objects, and rose unsteadily into the air.

'There.' Hoskins paused the film. He moved right up to the screen and pointed 'See this?'

'What are we looking for?' Stoker asked.

'Do you see this grey haze forming over the table?' Hoskins asked eagerly. 'Keep an eye on it.' He went back and started the film again.

Now that his attention had been drawn to it, Dawson could make out a smoky, almost man-shaped, blur surrounding the table. The footage continued, showing a startled Conway. Clapping, Chartair walked back into shot. He said a few words to Weizak but it was still clear from the look on his face that he suspected some kind of trickery.

Hoskins continued his commentary.

'Now Max is challenging Weizak to levitate *him*. You can see he still didn't believe any of it.'

Dawson and Stoker watched as the broad grin on the presenter's face rapidly turned to fear as he rose at least ten feet into the air. Conway staggered back, gawping in disbelief. Weizak himself had a look of intense concentration and was beginning to tremble, as though in the early stages of an epileptic fit.

Limbs flailing, Chartair was clearly screaming. For about twenty seconds, he remained suspended in mid-air before being lowered awkwardly to the floor.

The film abruptly ended.

Dawson and Stoker exchanged glances, wondering just what they were supposed to have seen, apart from the obvious impossibility of Weizak's demonstration. Admittedly, it could have been staged and illusionists throughout time had reputedly performed similar feats, from the fakirs of India to Harry Houdini. However, Chartair and Conway's reactions appeared absolutely genuine and the subsequent events had to be taken into account, for here was a potential explanation, however hard to accept, of how the three murders could have been committed.

'Did you see it?' Hoskins asked eagerly.

'You mean that smoke? Yeah, I think so,' Stoker answered. 'What was that?'

'That's what I wondered. At first, I thought it was part of the damage to the film but then I looked at the footage, frame by frame.' Hoskins turned the light on, carefully removed the reel from the projector and searched through the images. 'Here, look at this section.' He held a portion of film up to the light.

Dawson and Stoker crowded in to see.

Chartair was partially obscured by a grey-black mist, within which glared what, admittedly with a little imagination, could have been a pair of red eyes.

'What is that?' Stoker asked curiously.

'I don't know, but it appears in all the frames where Max was off the ground.' Hoskins revealed the rest of the film, showing where the ethereal image began and ended.

One of the frames was particularly clear and Dawson could make out what looked like smoky arms wrapped around Char-tair. 'Do you remember seeing this at the time?'

'I'm certain there was nothing there when it happened, which makes it all the weirder. And if I hadn't seen it, surely one of the others would've?' Hoskins pointed at the film. 'Somehow that *thing* showed up on this. Don't ask me how.'

'Could someone have added this to the film after it was shot?' Stoker asked.

'Impossible! I was there when it was developed and it hasn't left this room from the moment I viewed it. Anyway, I don't think it would be possible. I've some experience with special effects and I don't know of anyone who can do something that looks like that.' Hoskins was fumbling in a pocket for a pack of cigarettes but saw it was empty. He gratefully accepted one from Stoker and took a deep drag, inhaling the smoke to the very bottom of his lungs.

'How much do you know about what happened after this footage breaks off?' Dawson asked.

'Larry came storming down from the

gallery and ordered everybody off the set. All except Max, Randall and Jimmy.'

'*Jimmy?*' Dawson queried for clarification.

'Jimmy Hansby. He was the stage manager. So we went over to the canteen and we were all talking about what we'd seen. Some folk were certain it was a put-up job. Then the fire alarms went off. The whole place was evacuated and the fire trucks turned up. I went home pretty tired and figured we'd have some kind of explanation from Larry the next day.'

'And did you?'

'Yeah. He sent out a memo to the crew saying that Weizak was just a prankster and that there had been trouble with the electrics. We were paid off and he'd let us know when filming would start again. I didn't think any more of it until . . . ' Hoskins gestured helplessly to the reel of film.

'Did you say earlier that you tried to show this to Mr Hamilton?' Dawson asked.

'As soon as I saw it. But he refused to meet me. Said it was all a hoax and he wanted to forget about it. Wanted to forget about paying, if you ask me. A hundred thousand dollars is a lot of money, even for him.' Hoskins had calmed down a little as he told his tale but he was still jumpy.

'Have you been in contact with any one from the programme?' Dawson asked, wondering if Hoskins had become a complete recluse in recent weeks. The state of his living conditions; the many empty pizza boxes and discarded beer cans was proof, if any was needed, that the man had not been coping well. In which case, it was highly likely that he knew nothing about the three deaths.

'No. Not after Larry told me to get lost. I've been trying to call Jimmy for a couple of weeks but I get no answer. I thought about going round to see him but, to tell you the truth, I haven't left the house for . . . well, I can't remember how long. I daren't go out.' Hoskins sucked the last traces of nicotine out of his cigarette.

Seeing the state that the cameraman was in, Dawson considered the wisdom of informing him about the fates that had befallen the others. He reluctantly decided it would be unethical *not* to tell him. 'Mr Hoskins, I'm afraid I have some bad news — '

'Oh Christ! I knew it! Jimmy's . . . dead, isn't he?'

'I'm afraid so. As are Larry Hamilton and Max Chartair,' Dawson admitted.

Hoskins' jaw dropped and he slumped onto the sofa. 'This has to be a nightmare. It's just not real! And what about Randall? Is he still alive?'

'Missing,' Stoker said, laconically.

'Maybe he's got away then. God, I hope so.' Hoskins was shaking. 'This is all because Larry reneged on the deal, isn't it? It has to be. He should have just coughed up the cash. Hell, he would have made a mint from a genuine display of psychic talent. The stupid, short-sighted bastard! He could've made millions.'

'Why do you think he didn't?' Dawson asked.

'I don't know. Could be a matter of pride. Larry and Max had taken an instant dislike to Weizak. He looked like a bum; a weirdo. Most people at least make an effort to make themselves presentable for the camera but this guy stank and probably hadn't changed his clothes for months. I'd say that Larry freaked out and just reacted on instinct. Hell, who wouldn't?'

'Conway, for one, from what we've heard,' Stoker said.

Hoskins sighed. 'Yeah. I didn't really know Randall that well but he was really into his job. He used to be a stage magician; sleight of hand, all that stuff. He knew all the tricks of the trade. It made him ideal for sniffing out the fraudsters. I'm sure that he was convinced that Weizak had powers. Could be that's why he hasn't turned up dead yet. Then again, maybe he's found a way to protect himself.'

'Protect himself?' Dawson asked.

'From . . . from Weizak and that *thing* he controls.' Hoskins looked at Stoker. 'Any chance of another cigarette?'

Wordlessly, Stoker passed one over.

Hoskins lit up and stared earnestly at his two visitors. 'I can't carry on like this.

I'll go nuts. I keep seeing that mist at the corner of my eyes but I'm too scared to turn and look at it.'

Dawson nodded. 'The FBI would be happy to offer you a safe place to stay until we've apprehended the killer.'

Hoskins took a deep, unsteady breath. 'That'd be good, yeah. Somewhere a *long* way away.'

'I'll need to take the film with me,' Dawson said. 'And we'll take a formal statement from you in due course but I think our priority should be to get you out of here.' He turned his attention to Stoker. 'Can you help Mr Hoskins get a few things together while I call the Bureau?'

'Okay,' Stoker agreed. 'Let's pick up the necessities.' He ushered the dazed cameraman out of the room, focusing the man's attention on practicalities.

Dawson stood alone in the room with the reel of film. He maintained a strong degree of scepticism about the entire investigation but the images captured on the film had unsettled him. In his opinion, Hoskins was close to a breakdown and no wonder, given the circumstances. If the images they had seen were truly real, then most of what people thought they knew about reality was wrong. Pushing the enormity of the possibility to the back of his mind, he chose to concentrate on solving the murders. Whatever the explanation, the fact remained that three men were dead and they had a prime suspect in Weizak. He picked up the reel of film and placed it carefully back in the can, tucked it under his arm and left the room.

★   ★   ★

The flight from Los Angeles to San Francisco normally took around an hour and a half but due to several delays Dawson and Stoker did not arrive until late afternoon the day after their interview with Hoskins. After a hurried bite to eat, they got a cab to the Bureau headquarters.

'Christ. Never thought I'd be back here again.' Stoker frowned at the grandiose pillared entrance. 'I don't think you were here the day I got kicked out but the memories aren't exactly good ones.'

'I was on an investigation in Colombia at the time but people were still talking about it when I got back. You created a bit of a storm, I was told,' Dawson replied.

'I wasn't in the mood to go quietly. Not my style.' Stoker shook his head. 'Okay, let's get this over with.'

They entered the building and proceeded quickly to the Deputy Director's office. A few heads turned and there were some snide comments muttered as Stoker walked by. Dawson knocked on the door and they went in.

'You're late!' McMasters complained, looking pointedly at his watch.

'Yeah, and you're bald,' Stoker shot back disrespectfully.

A smile creased McMasters' face. 'Nice to see you too, Vincent. How goes the Satanism? They say it's thriving in LA.'

'I wouldn't know.' Casually, the private investigator lit a cigarette and took a drag before blowing out a cloud of smoke. 'I'm a Luciferian.'

'Whatever. I've heard all about your *Dirty Harry* antics down in Tinseltown.

Shooting people dead in the street, blowing up a freeway, rescuing voluptuous women.' McMasters read from a report on his desk. 'And what's this . . . extracting information through torture? A bit over the top, even by your trigger-happy standards, wouldn't you say?'

Stoker gave a nonchalant shrug. 'I guess a man's gotta do what a man's gotta do. Beats sitting behind a desk and pushing a pen around all day.'

McMasters chuckled. 'Well my time's short, so down to business. Dawson, I want a full update on the case. All the details.'

Over the next hour, Dawson and Stoker took McMasters through every twist of the investigation, ending with the three of them poring over the images on the reel of film.

'Do you really think this hasn't been falsified?' McMasters asked incredulously, scrutinising the weird mist.

'Not according to Hoskins and he'd probably recognise tampering,' Dawson replied.

'So what's your gut instinct? Do you

173

believe this guy has supernatural powers?' McMasters asked bluntly.

'I think I'd have to see it myself to be sure but I definitely think we need to factor in the possibility to any plans we make,' Dawson answered. He and Stoker had been talking it over on the flight and both realised that they were more than half-way convinced. 'Either we propose that someone went to extreme lengths to fake abilities, lengths that we have to bend over backwards to account for, or we accept that something that we thought to be impossible is, in fact, possible.'

'Okay.' McMasters nodded. 'I can go along with that, for now. So, Randall Conway is still missing, presumably in hiding. Our chief suspect is still at large and we've no idea where he may be. We *do* have a witness to one of the events safely stowed away and we have one lead — the letter from Wilder. I've been asking around about him and by all accounts he's a tricky character. There hasn't been any activity reported from his commune for at least a year but that means nothing. God knows what they're doing out there in the desert. Could be up to all sorts. Then again . . . they could all be dead.'

'Really our only course of action is to get in touch with Wilder; find out what that note was referring to. See if he has any idea where Conway might be holed up. The file I saw in the LA office clearly indicated that any contact has to be cleared so we'll need you to authorise it, sir,' Dawson said.

'I can do that. Sounds as though we've got good reason.' McMasters picked up the copy of the *Bardo Thodol* and opened it at a random page, wincing at what he saw. 'I really hope that none of this stuff has anything to do with the case. Christ, it's weird enough as it is. I could cope with a bit of ESP or whatever it is but not this mumbo-jumbo.' He flicked to another page and then saw that there were two stuck together. Idly, he prised them apart and then paused, eyes widening. 'This, however, is rather worrying.' He turned the book round so that the others could see and pointed to an illustration of a robed sorcerer within a magic circle. Stood in front of him, shadow-like, was a vaporous, anthropo-morphic entity.

The three men regarded the image in silence for a moment.

'Hmm.' Stoker rubbed his stubbled chin. 'A bit of a coincidence?'

'I'd say so,' Dawson agreed.

'I think it's crucial you go and see what Wilder knows about this,' said McMasters. 'If we're lucky, he'll hold the key to this business. Obviously, proceed with caution. I'll admit, I haven't read much about him but from what I've heard, he's either an out and out fraudster or someone who fervently believes all this rubbish. Either way, there's little doubt that he could be dangerous. And bear in mind, even if he's just in this for the money, it's quite likely that his followers are complete nutcases.'

'Talking of nutcases, if we *do* track Weizak down, what then?' Dawson asked. 'The LAPD are actively looking for him and they might get lucky. If he *can* do these kinds of things, what should our strategy be?'

'I say we shoot him,' Stoker said. 'Job done.'

'We don't actually know he's the murderer,' Dawson retorted.

'Oh come on!' Stoker exclaimed. 'He's got the motive — they screwed him over and judging by what's on that film, he's got the means. Unusual weapon of choice, I'll admit, but my mind's made up.'

'And exactly what evidence do you have to link Weizak with any of the scenes of crime?' Dawson argued.

'There's the car. We have circumstantial evidence to tie him to that,' Stoker countered.

'That's not going to stand up in court,' Dawson reasoned. 'Huh! I wonder if any of this will.'

'Which brings me back to the shooting option.' Stoker folded his arms. 'Someone like that's far too dangerous to — '

'I want Weizak brought in alive!' McMasters interrupted. 'Wounded would be acceptable but nothing fatal.' He paused for a moment. 'Have you stopped to think of the ramifications of all this? There are scientists on the other side of the Iron Curtain who are doing their damnedest to harness individuals with powers such as this man may possess . . . and, from what I've seen I've reason to believe that they're having some success. Now, I don't need to tell you the potential advantages to having someone with Weizak's capabilities working for us. If what you've been piecing together is true, he hasn't hurt any innocent bystanders. He's targeting a specific group of people who wronged him. Consequently, he may be amenable to some kind of deal.'

'Can we let three; maybe four murders go completely unpunished?' Dawson frowned.

'If the gain to national security is big enough . . . then, hell yes!' McMasters answered, emphatically.

8

The Dweller in the Desert

After three hours of driving, Dawson and Stoker had gone over every possible permutation of the investigation and had lapsed into a companionable silence. They had set off from San Francisco directly after an early breakfast and had soon left the well-travelled roads behind them.

As each mile of the lonely desert highway passed by, Dawson found his mind kept returning to the images from the *Bardo Thodol* which currently resided in his holdall on the back seat of the car. McMasters had got the entire book photographed and was hoping to get an expert opinion on it. The Deputy Director had agreed for them to take the original as a passport in order to gain an audience with Wilder, if such were needed. From the information they had gleaned, Wilder was unlikely to be well-disposed to anything he viewed as threatening — such as a visit from the authorities. God only knew what secrets he had to hide.

It was extremely hot and dry and there was hardly any traffic, making driving easy.

His stylish sunglasses on, Dawson took in the largely featureless landscape with interest. The desert had a feeling of isolation and timelessness that captured his imagination. This was as far from the modern, chaotic city-life of San Francisco or Los Angeles as one could get. Maybe it was easier to believe the unbelievable out here. He found his mind drifting to a time, just over a year ago, when he had helped bring to justice a South African conman who had concealed his money-laundering business behind a smoke-screen of New Age evangelism. The ministry that he had set up had been based in a place not unlike this. The fraudster had claimed that God had bestowed upon him the ability to perform miracles and his legion of devotees had willingly embraced his lies. Thousands and thousands of dollars had circulated as the gullible had gone to great lengths to receive his worthless blessings. In the end, it had all turned out to be a racket for the West Coast Mafia. It had been dangerous but certainly not as weird as his current case was proving to be.

They stopped at a remote gas station to refuel and get a cup of coffee.

'So, how do you want to do this?' said Stoker, lighting a cigarette.

Dawson set down his cup. 'Cautiously. First things first, this is a fact-finding mission. It's still possible that Wilder is unrelated to all of this. And the last thing we want to do is stir up unnecessary trouble. We can certainly ask him about the book and what kind of contact he's had with Conway. After all, it doesn't make much sense that a self-styled prophet gets in touch with a professional sceptic. There's obviously something strange going on.'

'Strange doesn't begin to cover what I've seen this past week,' Stoker responded.

'Even with your religious beliefs?'

'People just get it all wrong.' Stoker leaned forward, more animated than he had been so far that morning. 'I mean, it's not so much a belief in Lucifer as a physical being but rather as a concept. If anything, it's about belief in yourself. For a long time I felt guilty at still being alive when Annie and Elizabeth were killed. I thought not only that I couldn't, but that I *shouldn't* enjoy life any more. There's not a single day that passes that I don't miss them but the Church taught me that I do have a right to pursue my own personal happiness. Okay, it cost me my job but I gained a lot as well. Back in *The Black Oyster Bar* you asked me if I was happy. The honest answer is *no* — but I might be one day.'

Dawson nodded in agreement. 'I'm not religious at all but I can respect that. Certainly more than I can the Maurice Goldberg's of this world.'

'Exactly! That murderous bastard claims to be one of the 'Almighty's Beloved Disciples' but what was he going to do? Burn an innocent woman alive at the stake, and put it on TV no less! And the worst of it is that there are thousands of people who would have watched it and proclaimed it as God's work!' Stoker's expression grew dark. 'And yet, according to most of my fellow countrymen, people like *me* are dangerous!'

Smiling wryly, Dawson mulled things over for a moment. 'So, what do you make of all these strange, doomsday cults? They seem to be springing up all over the place nowadays.'

'I think people are scared. And who can blame them? After all, there's a lot to be scared about; nuclear annihilation, the ongoing oil crisis, environmental issues, terrorism, drugs, social unrest, political and economic uncertainty. It's small wonder the faithful are proclaiming the End Days will soon be upon us.'

Dawson checked his wristwatch. 'Come on. Time to get moving. From the map there's still another sixty miles or so to go.'

★ ★ ★

It was early afternoon when Dawson saw the barely noticeable and un-signposted, tumbleweed-strewn, cacti-bordered track that wound its way into the rocky hinterland. Slowing down, he turned onto it.

After a short distance, they began to notice that in several places along either side of the route, posts had been set up atop of which were horned, bovine skulls, some of which bore curious red and yellow painted sigils. Proceeding further, clearing a low rise, they saw in a large depression before them a disorderly arrangement of small, rusty and ramshackle hangar-like buildings, many constructed from mismatched sheets of corrugated iron. Scattered around were several unroadworthy-looking vehicles — coaches for the main but also some battered cars, jeeps and motorbikes. Around this makeshift compound had been erected a perimeter fence of barbed wire; further fortified with a lookout tower. Two crude electricity pylons — on opposing sides of the enclosure — and the loud crackling sound now audible gave ample warning that a formidable ring of electricity circulated the area.

'It looks like some kind of defunct military base,' Stoker remarked. 'A 1950s nuke shelter, perhaps?'

'I think we walk from here,' said Dawson, bringing the car to a halt and switching off the engine. He picked up the holdall in which was the *Bardo Thodol*, checked that his gun was in its holster and got out as did Stoker.

Trying to look unthreatening, they made their way forward, hoping that their progress was not being observed through the sight of a telescopic rifle.

A man emerged from one of the low buildings by the side of the gate. He was bearded, long-haired with a green bandana wound around his head, scrawny and bare chested. A handgun was tucked into the waistband of his torn and faded denims.

Approaching the entrance, Dawson noticed that it was a typical metal swing gate, reinforced with a hotchpotch of miscellaneous pieces of junk; a car tyre, several dustbin lids, and an obviously purloined freeway sign. All of these had been arcanely decorated with spray paint in strange swirls and patterns.

The crackling electricity was charging the hot, desert air, creating the smell of ozone.

'You lost?' The scruffy, hirsute gatekeeper queried, his tone adversarial.

'I hope not. I'm here to see the Prophet. I've heard a lot about him,' Dawson answered calmly. Now that he was up close and personal, he could see the tell-tale signs of heavy drug use in the other's eyes. Casually, he took off his sunglasses and returned them to an inner jacket pocket.

'Don't bullshit me! You're cops. We don't like cops here. In fact, we don't like anyone who turns up uninvited. Take my advice — turn around, get back in your car and don't ever come back here.' The gatekeeper's eyes narrowed. 'Do that and you might find you live longer.'

Dawson was unperturbed by the air of menace. 'If you want to do it that way, fine. But bear this in mind — one call from me and the FBI will tear this place apart. As it happens, I'm not particularly interested in you lot or what you get up to but if Derek Wilder's inside, I want a word with him.'

The mention of Wilder's name clearly had an effect.

Much of the gatekeeper's bravado slipped away. 'Wait here,' he muttered before walking quickly to the largest of the buildings. He returned a few minutes later, accompanied by an older, extremely slim man in an ochre robe. His completely bald head shone in the sunlight, the forehead so high that the skull appeared to be domed. It was unmistakably Wilder, or Haggai the Prophet as he currently called himself.

'Okay. You work on him and I'll keep an eye out for any funny business,' Stoker whispered.

Wilder approached the gate, arms wide. Then, stretching his lips back over his teeth, he spoke, his voice coming out in a sort of sibilant hiss. 'Greetings gentlemen! Seekers of knowledge are always welcome here. Please, tell me how we can help you.'

'I've reason to believe that Randall Conway has visited you recently, indeed may still be here.' Now that he had met the man, Dawson had to acknowledge that there was a certain aura about Wilder, due to both his unusual physical appearance and his almost mesmeric tone of voice. He was suddenly and vividly reminded of the character *Kaa* in the film version of *The Jungle Book* he had been to see with his young nephew a few years ago. Given also the slightly reptilian cast to Wilder's features, the resemblance bordered on the uncanny.

'That is correct. Mr Conway has been my guest for a few days now. Is that a problem? I assure you, I'm not keeping him here against his will,' said Wilder.

Dawson felt a surge of relief. 'I'm not suggesting you are, Mr Wilder. However, I do need to speak to him on a matter of some urgency.' He could see that other figures were now appearing on the scene — more spaced-out, blank-eyed hippies for the most part but there were a few who looked worryingly focused and distinctly dangerous. Several of them carried rifles. If things were to turn nasty then the odds were clearly stacked against them.

'I'm afraid that's a bit of a problem. You see, Mr Conway has come to us for a rest — a retreat. He particularly asked *not* to be disturbed and I must honour that request.' Wilder spoke calmly but once or twice his eyes flicked to the road stretching out behind the two investigators. 'I'm sure you understand that people sometimes need to find a special haven from the cares and burdens of modern life. What we offer here is tranquillity — understanding and the means to become more enlightened beings. I can of course convey any message you may have for him . . . that is, after his time of seclusion has elapsed.'

Dawson could see that Wilder was preparing to dismiss them, forcibly if necessary but he had one last card to play. 'That's a real shame. You see, I was hoping to deliver an old book I believe he might be glad to receive.'

The words hit home. Wilder's eyes widened slightly and his composure faltered. 'A book, you say?' he asked.

'The *Bardo Thodol*, I think it's called,' Dawson said casually but he was watching Wilder like a hawk, knowing that a signal from the cult leader could easily start an attack. He was betting that the book was important to the man in some way or other and just hoped that the weirdo did not want it so badly that he would simply shoot them to get it. The Bureau knew where they were of course and retribution would follow but it would be too late for the two of them.

Wilder seemed to reach a decision. 'You have the book with you?' he asked, his dark, oval-shaped eyes on the holdall Dawson had slung over a shoulder.

'Yes and I'm happy to give it to Mr Conway,' Dawson answered. 'In person.'

'Very well. Given the circumstances, I believe Mr Conway would forgive the intrusion. I must ask you to do just as I say, though, for your own safety. Our security system is . . . *unusual*.' Wilder pulled back from the gate and gave a few muttered orders to the gun-toting gatekeeper who walked over to the nearest shack.

'Well, that worked. Still, I wouldn't trust this lot as far as I could throw them. And, Christ, is he weird or what?' Stoker asked in a hushed voice. He swatted at a large fly that had landed on the nape of his neck.

Surreptitiously, Dawson nodded in agreement.

'Okay gentlemen,' Wilder said. 'When I open the gate you must walk straight in and make quite sure not to touch any part of the metal.' He signalled to the gatekeeper and pressed a button.

The gates swung wide.

Cautiously, Dawson and Stoker stepped inside.

A few seconds later the gate closed behind them.

'What's with the electricity?' Stoker asked.

'Just a means of discouraging any un-welcome guests; coyotes, mountain lions, bobcats and such,' Wilder answered.

'You have a lot of trouble with those out here?' Stoker questioned.

'On occasion,' Wilder answered but his attention was fixed on Dawson's holdall. 'Could I just have a look at the book?' he asked, reaching out.

'No,' Dawson said firmly. 'We want to see Mr Conway.'

'Of course. I'll take you to him. This way, if you please.' Wilder led Dawson and Stoker into the largest of the ramshackle buildings. Piles of junk took up much of the floor space. There were broken metal bedframes, a couple of broken television sets, a heap of old tyres and several stripped-down vehicles.

Wrench in hand, a female mechanic, her clothes grimy and oil-spattered, was tinkering with one such rust-bucket, her long hair tied back with a greasy rag. She looked up. There was no friendliness in her eyes; no signs of acknowledgement at seeing strangers — just a vacuous blankness.

Wilder opened a door. Beyond which was a small, not particularly safe-looking lift. He pulled open the grilled gate, waited for his 'guests' to step inside, closed the gate and then pulled a lever.

For a long moment nothing happened.

Dawson and Stoker exchanged bemused glances.

Then, with a strong judder and the clanking sound of the winch mechanism, the lift began to descend.

It was crammed, hot and claustrophobic.

With a bump, the lift soon came to a stop.

Wilder opened the gate and stepped out.

They found themselves in a subterranean hallway. The walls were hewn from the desert rock and lines of cables, pipes and some form of rudimentary ventilation system could be clearly seen. At the far end was a huge, metal, circular, bank vault type door. It looked solid and impenetrable — the kind of thing that had been installed in order to provide shielding against an atomic blast.

'I sometimes see this door, as indeed I see all doors, as an allegory of the mind,' Wilder said enigmatically as he stepped up towards it. 'You can get out easily enough but only a few of us have the know-how to get in.' He punched in a six-figure combination on a pad, then pressed a large red button.

Dawson did not respond, his mind temporarily swimming, wondering for a moment if there was something profound in what the other had just said. He felt a prickle of sweat break out on his forehead. Cautiously, he flexed his fingers, tensed the muscles of his shoulders. He strained his eyes in order to see into the long shadows which seemed deeper and longer down here. He was still expecting trouble and thought about reaching for his gun as the huge door swung slowly open to reveal a large, cavernous area beyond, from which several less-imposing closed doors lead off. Each door had a plain sign on it — kitchen; dormitories; restrooms; armoury; mess hall and sanctuary.

Wilder opened the door to the sanctuary.

They entered a narrow passageway. The walls were decorated with those strange symbols and talismans that had festooned the main gate to the compound and looked as though they had only recently been applied. At the far end was yet another vault-like door.

'What's all this in aid of?' Stoker could not help but ask.

'I think I'll save the explanation until Mr Conway can contribute,' Wilder said over his shoulder. 'He's just through here.' Tapping in another security code, he unlocked the metal portal and stepped into a large, domed room.

A man who had been sitting on a bench sprang to his feet. 'Who are they? What's happening?' he demanded angrily of Wilder.

Dawson recognised Randall Conway, but only just. The renowned psychic debunker had the beginnings of a scruffy beard, dirty clothes and a wild look in his eyes. 'Hello, Mr Conway. I've brought something for you,' he said, reaching into his holdall and holding out the book.

Conway dashed forward to grab it, snatching it from Dawson's hand. 'Tuska Grembi's *Bardo Thodol!* Thank God!' Tears welled in his eyes as he hugged the book to his chest as though it were a long-lost friend.

★   ★   ★

Over the course of the next hour or so, Dawson and Stoker were told one of the most incredible stories they had ever heard; one that tested their credulity to the limits yet at the same time validated much of what they had pieced together. For, if their informants were to be believed, and the footage shown to them by Hoskins strongly supported them, several months ago, Andrei Weizak *had* featured on *Chartair's Challenge*. He had purported to possess telekinetic abilities, and had been given his opportunity to prove his claim in order to scoop the prize money. As specified by the rules of the show, he had been tested under laboratory conditions and the talents he had demonstrated had been truly amazing.

After having been searched to ensure that he had no concealed magnets or wires, Weizak repeatedly raised and lowered a series of miscellaneous objects by the power of his mind alone.

The reaction amongst the crew had been mixed, for whereas Conway had been deeply impressed but keen to test Weizak further, Chartair and Hansby had been dismissive and defensive. Chartair, in particular, had taken an instant dislike to the 'pinko, long-haired hippy' and had fully intended to make a mockery of his claims. When confronted with what, on the surface, looked an authentic demonstration of psychic ability, the presenter had immediately decided to set another challenge — demanding that Weizak use his telekinetic powers to levitate *him*.

To the surprise of all, Weizak had obliged.

Suspended in mid-air, ten feet off the ground, Chartair, screaming to be let down, had shouted curses at Weizak while Hansby and Conway stared in disbelief.

Weizak had set Chartair back on the ground. Palm extended and a broad grin on his face, he had asked for the prize money.

It was at that point that a white-faced Hamilton had come down from the control room. Calling Hansby, Chartair and Conway into a hasty conference, he had asserted that on no account would they be paying out. There was no fund set aside for it and he was damned if he was going to spend his own money on someone who, contrary to what Chartair now definitely believed, was nothing more than a low-down trickster. Ignoring protestations from Conway and Chartair that there was no explanation other than this being real, Hamilton started to make accusations, even going so far as to suggest that Chartair and Weizak were in cahoots and would split the prize money.

What happened then erased any lingering doubts as to the veracity of Weizak's claims. The door to the room had been torn off its hinges, revealing the furious figure of the 'contestant'. It was obvious that he had overheard their heated exchange and, clearly angered at the outcome, had decided to now vent his wrath.

Chaos erupted.

Hamilton was thrown backwards by an invisible force and raised up to the ceiling, his hands clasping at his throat. With nothing more than a stare, Weizak upended the table and hurled it against Hansby. From outside the room there had come a crash as a lighting gantry fell to the floor and moments later the piercing trill of the fire alarm had sounded. It was at that point that Weizak had broken off his attack and opted to make an escape, leaving the burning studio. Everyone had got out but the show had been shut down. Conway had not known what to make of the whole affair but had been horrified when Hansby had died not long after.

'There were some very strange rumours going round about Hansby's death and when I started asking the right people, I realised that Weizak must be behind it. I got talking to a groundskeeper over in Huntersville and he told me about how his body was found,' Conway revealed. 'There's no doubt Weizak is set on killing us all for cheating him.'

'I'm afraid you may be right,' Dawson said. 'Larry Hamilton and Max Chartair are both dead.'

Conway moaned.

'What I want to know is where on earth did he get these powers?' Stoker inquired.

'From me,' answered Wilder calmly.

'*From you!?*' Dawson exclaimed. He had half-expected there to be a connection between Weizak and Wilder but to hear it confirmed still came as a surprise.

'Andrei was one of my acolytes. One who held great potential,' Wilder revealed.

'Care to expand on that?' Dawson asked.

Wilder smiled. 'When I first met him he was a sad case — an unsuccessful thief and a drifter; a lowlife floating aimlessly through the weave of existence. He liked the idea of what I could offer him — that I could steer him in the true direction and for the first few years he was with us he was a valued member of the *Children of Haggai*. As time went on, however, he became restless. It's a classic case of the apprentice hungering for knowledge from the master before he is ready for it.'

'Get to the point, Mr Wilder,' said Stoker impatiently. 'What *are* these powers?'

'As you wish.' Wilder crossed his arms. 'The Tibetan monks call the phenomenon a *tulpa* — a thought-form. My research over the years has led me to realise that this ability has emerged in different places, at different times. The ancient Egyptians and the Incas used it in their vast building projects, whilst in Europe, throughout the Middle Ages; it was mistaken for possession by demonic forces. This is not a new science, gentlemen, but rather, a very old one. It may be better if I demonstrate . . . may I borrow a pen?'

Wordlessly, Dawson removed a pen from his jacket pocket and handed it over.

Wilder held the pen and delicately balanced it upright on the palm of his left hand. He then removed his right hand from the pen, which started to spin and then, to Dawson and Stoker's astonishment, it wrote the word 'Believe' on the prophet's skin.

Clearly impressed, Dawson took the pen back. He examined it curiously, checking to see if there was anything unusual about it. 'Okay, you've convinced me.'

'The *tulpa*, certainly as I understand it, and please bear in mind that I am but a lay theosophist, allows the practitioner to extend his metaphysical reach beyond his corporeal form. It's taken me over thirty years to control my emotions, which fuel the psychic power, enabling me to channel it and make it into a force capable of physical interaction. In addition to which, I have never sought to use it to destroy. Andrei, unfortunately, is *ruled* by his negative emotions and has become an unstable, unhappy, capricious man, who I have to say has been wronged by many people. He is a deeply troubled individual who I was trying to help. Now, hurt and bitterness flow through him unchecked. His thirst for revenge is unlikely to be satiated until Mr Conway here is also dead, or unless he himself dies.'

'This *tulpa* or whatever it's called, does it take the form of a sort of smoky, man-shaped outline?' Stoker asked.

'Accounts vary,' Wilder replied. 'It is extremely rare for a *tulpa* to manifest in any visible form except in times of great need. My own mentor was able to do some extraordinary things when he called forth his *tulpa*. In Kwam-Qua, a remote village in the foothills of the Himalayas, I saw him divert the course of a river but even this feat did not result in a visible being — a haze, nothing more.'

'We have reason to believe that this *tulpa* was caught on film. On certain frames — ' Dawson began.

'*On film!* You mean some of it survived?' Conway asked eagerly.

'Only a few minutes but it's pretty convincing,' Dawson answered.

'Finally!' Conway sank back onto his chair. 'I finally have proof!' His face broke into an excited smile.

'Well that's great, but with Weizak out to kill you I think you have other priorities,' Stoker said.

Instantly, the smile on Conway's face vanished as the reality of his plight hit home.

Dawson stood up. 'We can get you to a place of safety. One of our most secret and defended locations could be ready and prepared for you within hours.'

Conway stared at the FBI Special Agent in surprise. 'You want me to leave?' he asked incredulously.

'Do you not realise that until Weizak is safely in custody you are at risk?' Dawson said.

'That's exactly why I came here!' Conway retorted. 'What can *you* do to protect me from someone with powers like that?'

'We have defences here, which is why Mr Conway, who visited us a few years ago as part of his research, appealed for my help,' Wilder added.

'The electric fence?' Stoker asked.

'Exactly. Strong electro-magnetic fields are inimical to the emanations of someone using these kind of powers. I have tested it myself and if I try any kind of psychic manipulation by the charged field I receive quite a shock; the jolt was powerful enough to knock me off my feet. I believe it will prevent Weizak from effecting anything inside the compound.'

'You said there's something in the *Bardo Thodol* that can stop him,' Conway prompted hopefully.

'I believe there is.' Wilder took the book from Conway, set it down on the table and turned through the pages, quickly finding the one he sought. 'Yes. Here it is. An incantation that neutralises a practitioner.'

'So you can read that?' Stoker asked.

'The book would be of little use if I couldn't,' Wilder answered measuredly.

'And will it work?' Dawson asked.

'I believe so.' Wilder nodded.

'Then let's waste no time. Do it! Recite the incantation!' Conway said frantically. 'Weizak could be here at any time! He's tracked the others down and he's been after me for days. I've been driving round California trying to keep one step ahead of him but I felt his presence wherever I went, and then I came here — the only place that might offer me protection.'

'All this talk of spells and stuff . . . why not just shoot the bastard?' suggested Stoker, going for what he considered to be the easy and pragmatic approach. 'Or are you going to tell me that he's immune to bullets?'

'It's entirely possible that his aura could be strong enough to deflect bullets,' Wilder said. 'I've seen such things done before. And then there's his *tulpa*. It is an incredibly powerful force capable of physical interaction. Before he left, Andrei had already mastered the ability to project his will in such a manner that he could levitate heavy objects. By the sounds of it, he's progressed even further now.'

Dawson looked at Conway. 'Well, I guess it's your choice. You can either come with us or you can stay here. I know which I'd do if I were in your position.'

9

'Blackbeard'

'The man's an idiot! A bloody nutcase! If he wants to die out there then let him!' Stoker inhaled the smoke from a cigarette as he gazed out of the open passenger window at the miles of rocky desert which stretched and shimmered like a mirage for as far as the eye could see. Apart from the rhythmic purr of the engine, the low sound of the tyres on the highway and the muted rumble of thunder on the southern horizon, there was an absolute quietness that, like the stifling heat, wrapped itself all around. Even the wind generated from the fast-moving car was hot and arid.

'He's misguided, certainly.' Dawson was disappointed. They had failed in convincing Conway to accompany them and he was well aware that he had little to no legal justification in taking him against his own will. Admittedly, his testimony would prove invaluable in getting some kind of a charge levelled at Weizak but just how far would all of this go in a court of law? All he could do now was return to headquarters and see how far, and in what direction, McMasters wanted things pursued.

'And so that's Wilder. One weird mother if you ask me. I don't suppose you saw inside that armoury — well, I got a glance as we passed by on the way out. They're building what looked like a flying saucer out of scavenged car parts down there. Not only that, but, in addition to the racks of machine-guns, there were also flame-throwers, grenades and rocket launchers.'

'Maybe they're preparing for World War Three.' A sensation of restless apprehension that had been growing in Dawson's mind since leaving the compound was now solidifying into something more definite, more urgent. It was as though the utter stillness and desolation around him was peopled with soundless, half-noticed things that flitted on the edge of his vision, moving swiftly and soundlessly in the silence. A sick sensation of impending disaster began to take hold of him, stirring in the far depths of his mind. Shaking his head, he tried to focus; to concentrate on driving.

'They're certainly equipped for it.' Stoker took a further drag from his cigarette, scanning the rugged terrain through keen eyes. Mostly barren and blindingly yellow-white in the harsh, mid-afternoon sunlight, the Mojave Desert looked as though it went on for ever. It was hard to believe that the casinos, the nightclubs, the strip-joints and the glitzy hotels of Las Vegas lay just several miles beyond the northern horizon.

'Don't worry, that'll go in my report.' Coming to a more traversable stretch of highway, Dawson shifted gears and stepped on the gas. 'So, have you any ideas as to what we do now?'

'Not sure, although I still reckon we should have stayed. I don't see how we're going to find Weizak otherwise.'

'I'm not sure that's such a good idea. There's no longer any doubt in my mind that he does possess supernatural powers.'

Stoker flicked his cigarette butt out of the window. 'What's your take on Wilder's claim that he could use some kind of spell against Weizak? It sounds far-fetched to me but, Christ, this whole thing is crazy.'

'That may have a chance of working. If this *tulpa*-thing is some ancient Tibetan mystical-magical ability then it seems . . . *logical* that an ancient Tibetan spell might counter it.'

Stoker shook his head. 'The way I see it, we've got *two* problems here. The first is finding Weizak and the other is bringing him in alive for McMasters. The only way I can think of solving the first problem is by using Conway as bait.' He turned and looked at Dawson. 'Don't tell me that hasn't crossed your mind.'

'Well, yes, I have considered that.'

'As to the second problem, I've got nothing.'

Dawson drove on in silence for a moment. 'Actually, I do have an idea about the second problem. It's something I've been thinking about.'

'Let's hear it.'

'What does Weizak want?'

'That's easy, revenge,' Stoker replied.

'So, what if we let him get his revenge

. . . and then make him an offer? Immunity from prosecution and the money he was owed.'

'Christ, Dawson! I thought *I* was the hard-hearted one. Are you just going to let him murder Conway?'

'It's only a suggestion; a last resort. Obviously we'll try every — ' Dawson stopped mid-sentence. 'Look at that!' His eyes were fixed on a point half a mile or so distant. 'It looks like a sandstorm . . . heading straight for us. It's moving fast!' He stepped on the brake pedal and started to decelerate, soon bringing the car to a halt.

Less than a minute later, there came the savage howling of the approaching wind. The sky changed colour. No longer was it a brilliant mirror, polished blue-white. Instead it was a dark, ominous hue; shadowy and filled with twisting, boiling shapes — a whirling cloud that moved rapidly towards them, scudding over the baking Badlands. It was as though night had come over the face of the desert in the middle of the day. An evil, hot, suffocating night, filled with whirlwinds of airborne grit and stinging sand.

Stoker wound up the window, his eyes fixed on the rapidly advancing grey-black cloud. 'What the hell is that? A dust devil?'

Dawson was about to respond when a dense, airborne particulate fell on the windscreen, soon obscuring all view and plunging them into darkness. Panic threatened to take hold and several seconds passed before he realised that he was holding his breath as though subconsciously fearful that whatever had caused this strange phenomenon was toxic in origin. He gulped nervously, only vaguely aware that his companion was fumbling with a box of matches.

Light from the small flickering flame cast Stoker's normally healthy-looking face into a ghastly pallor. Wide-eyed, he peered around him in the shadowy darkness that had descended.

There came the sound of a heavy thump on the car's roof.

'What the . . . ?' Stoker's match burnt out. Hastily, he struck another. No sooner had he done so when there came what sounded like the barefooted patter of small feet on the metal surface mere inches above his head. This was followed by a scrabbling commotion from his side of the van as though a pack of rats was trying to get in, prompting him to shrink back in his seat.

The noise shifted to under the vehicle.

Exchanging a worried glance with Stoker, Dawson drew his gun.

The unnerving sound ceased. Everything was quiet. Silence was like a lead blanket, pressing itself down tightly against them.

For a terrible moment, Dawson felt unable to breathe. It was as though he was suffocating from the fear. A numbing terror crept through his body, clutching at his heart. It was how he imagined being buried alive would feel. And those weird sounds. What had caused them? At any moment, he dreaded to see something pale and grotesque press itself up against the windscreen. He took several deep breaths, well aware that he was allowing his imagination to run riot. Mentally, he tried to put things into some kind of perspective; to restore reason and sanity.

It was just a sandstorm, nothing more — and yet he knew in his heart that he was wrong and that this was something else entirely.

There was a sudden, violent judder.

Both men yelled as the car rocked to one side. The side Stoker was on was raised higher.

The car then thumped back on to its tyres.

There came a resounding bang on the roof, strong enough to cause metal to crumple. The vehicle began to shake from side to side.

'It's a bloody earthquake!' Stoker shouted.

In his mind, Dawson imagined the car teetering on the edge of a freshly-opened fissure, the ground crumbling away as the earth threatened to swallow them down into its depths.

'We need to get out!' Stoker was reaching for the door handle when something cracked against the windscreen causing it to splinter. A ferocious blast struck the car with enough force to pitch it over to one side.

And then the vehicle was turning again.

Now upended, it canted dangerously, before crashing back down.

Blood trickled from a shallow cut on Dawson's forehead where he had hit the window and he was in pain from having been crushed by his companion. He now lay sprawled, uncomfortably pinioned against the steering wheel and the windscreen. His mind was screaming at him to get out, to escape from this madness. Futilely, he pushed at the door but it would not budge.

Groaning, Stoker managed to extricate his left foot which had become trapped under his seat. Cursing volubly, he shifted his position and kicked out at the windscreen. Savagely, he booted it again and again.

Dawson could smell petrol. He began to panic. Fear leant him strength and he too began to frantically hammer at the glass with the butt of his handgun, believing that the vehicle was liable to explode at any moment.

The darkness began to recede.

Splotches of bright, afternoon sunlight began to form on the cracked windscreen as, like melting ice, the pervasive gloom began to dissipate. Soon the black cloud and the nightmare it had brought in its wake had vanished completely. However, there was still the very real danger of the leaking petrol combusting.

'Come on! We're not out of this yet.' Dawson succeeded in shattering the windscreen. Knocking aside the remaining shards of glass, he crawled out, Stoker right behind him.

On bleeding hands and grazed knees, the two men dragged themselves further, before clambering to their feet and moving well clear of the overturned car.

Dawson's sunglasses were cracked and without them he had to shield his eyes against the harsh sunlight. There was nothing but death out there, of that he was certain. Hot, burning, agonising death — whether due to dehydration, starvation, sunstroke or a multitude of venomous insects and reptiles, in addition to whatever had wrought such terrible violence against his car. He knew that this was a harsh and unforgiving part of California, criss-crossed by hundreds of barely navigable trails that led to places no one sane would care to go. He stared out through slitted eyes across the trackless rugged wastes of the Mojave Desert. Everywhere, it was the same. It made no difference in which direction he turned his head. It was a scorching, mind shrivelling hell that stretched away and away towards a horizon that seemed to tilt and heave.

Wearily, both men made their way to a pile of boulders at the side of the road and sat down. From where they were, they could see the black cloud whirling like a tornado in the distance.

'Am I seeing things, or is it following the road?' Stoker remarked.

'Looks like it,' Dawson agreed. 'How much would you bet that Weizak's got something to do with that?'

'It's got to be him. *Shit!* What the hell are we going to do about this?' Stoker cursed. 'At least the car looks like it's not going to blow up but I can't see us getting it moving again in a hurry.'

'How far do you think we are from the compound? Ten miles? Fifteen?'

'Something like that. Too far to get there on foot, at least in this heat.' Stoker took out his gun, idly clicked out a magazine and counted his bullets. 'I could do with a drink. There's a double bourbon on the rocks in *The Black Oyster Bar* that's just waiting for me.'

Dawson cautiously approached the upturned car, wondering if they could find a way to right it and, if so, whether it could be started even then. He had little mechanical knowledge but they had to try something.

'Hang on a minute.' Stoker got to his feet and pointed. 'Could be we're in luck.'

Dawson squinted. He could no longer make out the unnatural dark vortex but, looking in the other direction; he saw the plume of dust indicative of an approaching vehicle. It became clearer and his spirits rose to see that it was a clapped-out pick-up truck. He stepped up to the roadside and raised an arm.

'Shame. I was hoping it'd be a coach-load of cheerleaders,' Stoker commented wryly as he put his gun away and joined Dawson.

The pick-up truck began to slow down.

As it drew nearer they could see just how much of a wreck it was. It was clearly a pre-war model which creaked and groaned in every seam, the engine wheezing terribly under the shaking bonnet as it swayed in a series of bone-jarring jolts from side to side. The fender was half-hanging off. Rust and over exposure to the elements had caused much of its paintwork to peel away like the skin sloughing off a rattlesnake. Grey-black smoke belched from its exhaust. Daubed in red paint on the side were the words *Blackbeard's Pest Control*.

The vehicle came to a halt less than ten yards away.

The driver's window was down and the placid, comforting strains of John Denver's *Take Me Home, Country Roads* came drifting out. The face that followed was less pleasant — ugly, bearded, fat and grinning inanely. The man's eyes were close-set and piggy and his nose was squashed and upturned so that it resembled a snout. Lengths of long black hair straggled from below the battered Stetson — which had a skull and crossbones design on it — the man sported. He wore a stained vest, a pair of grimy dungarees and thick leather boots. 'I see you guys been hit by that twister. Damn weirdest thing I ever seen. All along back-trail from Joshua Creek to the turnoff at Stump's Farm there's automobiles an' trucks all o'er the road. Some telegraph poles up an' all.' 'Blackbeard' finished off a can of *Budweiser*, crushed it in a meaty hand, and then tossed it onto the seat beside him where it joined a not inconsiderable pile of emptics.

'Forget the cheerleaders, I'd settle for someone normal-looking,' Stoker muttered, thinking to himself that if there was ever a contest for the ugliest man in the state then this guy would be a top contender.

Dawson nodded in tacit agreement. He took a few steps towards the vehicle. 'As you can see, we've been badly hit. We'd be grateful for a ride.'

'Where're ya headed?' 'Blackbeard' drawled.

'We need to get to a small ranch, back along the dirt track,' Dawson answered. 'I realise it's probably out of your way so I'm happy to make it worth your while.' He reached into his inside jacket pocket for his wallet and withdrew it. 'What do you say, ten dollars?'

'I'll do it for fifty,' the bearded stranger said promptly.

'Okay.' Dawson opened the wallet and began to pull the notes out.

The driver's eyes fixed greedily on the money. 'I meant seventy. Yeah, seventy . . . that sounds better.'

Stoker lost his patience. 'I know what sounds better.' He pulled out his gun and levelled it at the driver. 'You take us where we want to go and — '

'Yeah, an' ya can kiss ma ass!' 'Blackbeard' ducked down and sprung back up like a grotesque jack-in-the-box, a pump-action shotgun in his hands.

Stoker fired. The slug blew a chunk out of the morbidly obese man's shoulder, causing him to drop his weapon and scream in agony. Handgun at the ready, the private investigator stalked forward. Deaf to his victim's cries of pain, he kicked the pump-action shotgun under the vehicle, pulled open the driver's door, reached in, grabbed the four hundred and fifty pound unfortunate and, with some difficulty, hauled him out, manhandling him to the ground. In the fracas his opponent's hat came off and he was surprised to find that the man's hair was nothing but a wig to which it had been fastened. The pate underneath was lumpy, with an old, long surgical scar visible.

'Bastards! Sons o' bitches!' 'Blackbeard' shouted, bloody fingers clutched to his shoulder. Without his hair-piece he looked even more hog-like. 'I'll get ya for this! I'll have the law on ya!'

'We *are* the law,' Dawson said, displaying his FBI badge. 'And by the power invested in me I'm commandeering your vehicle.'

'Like hell ya are!' 'Blackbeard' tried to get to his feet but a swift kick from the private investigator prevented him from doing so. Groaning, he clutched his ribs.

'Don't try anything, fatso, or we'll leave you here to rot,' Stoker warned. 'I'll warrant there's enough pork on you to keep the buzzards fed for months.'

Dawson opened the passenger door of the pick-up truck and started to sweep out the mass of crumpled beer cans. It was as he was doing so that he inadvertently knocked against the glove compartment which sprung open. He turned to push it shut and then froze. Inside was a plastic bag filled with what were unmistakably human ears. He stared for a moment in disbelief then straightened up. 'Vincent?' he said quietly as he removed the bag. 'Take a look at this.'

Stoker came round. Chewing his bottom lip, he regarded the grisly trophies in silence. After a moment, he turned to Dawson. 'I think he deserves another bullet, don't you?'

'What're you bastards doin' in there? An' get yer hands off ma private property!' 'Blackbeard' shouted.

Bag of ears in hand, Dawson stood, looking down at the wounded man. 'Care to explain?'

'What's that? I've never seen that before,' 'Blackbeard' said unconvincingly.

'Don't lie.' Dawson's eyes were full of contempt. 'This was in your glove compartment. You, my friend, have got some serious questions to answer.'

'I told ya . . . ain't nothin' to do with me,' the ear collector protested.

Stoker had been searching for anything else incriminating. He came forward, holding a length of rope, a roll of duct tape and a ten-inch, serrated hunting knife — dried blood visible on its blade. 'And this? I take it this has nothing to do with you either?'

For a fat man, 'Blackbeard' made a relatively agile scramble for his pump-action shotgun.

Dawson had anticipated such a move. Delivering a hefty kick to the other, he then caught him around the neck and, exerting all of his strength, he pulled him away. After a curse-filled struggle and with Stoker's help, the two of them trussed their big, beer-bellied opponent and forced him, at gunpoint, up onto the back of the pick-up truck.

'Blackbeard' continued to kick and swear.

'I've had enough of this.' Rubbing his forehead, which had taken a punch in the melee, Stoker then drove in two firm jabs, both landing squarely on his prisoner's bristling jaw, knocking him out cold. Noticing a sheet of tarpaulin that was caked in dirt and old bloodstains, he draped it over the man, wound the rope around it, pulled it taut and fastened it.

'Are you ready for round two?' Dawson asked from where he sat behind the wheel.

Stoker gave a weary nod. Wincing in pain, he sat himself in the passenger seat. Grimacing, he picked up an ear that had fallen from the bag. 'This has been a very strange day . . . and something tells me it's going to get worse.'

★ ★ ★

The dilapidated pick-up truck found the long dirt road leading to Wilder's compound a challenge. A combination of bald tyres, poor suspension and a variety of worrying sounds from the engine made for an unpleasant journey. The only part of it that seemed to work properly was the radio.

As Dawson drove, Stoker finally found

the owner's driving license tucked away at the back of the glove compartment. 'Here we are. Jacob Tarrant. According to this, he's a resident of Barstow.'

'A bit of a drive from here,' Dawson said speculatively. 'Wonder what brought him out here?'

'Christ knows, but this desert would be a good place to hide bodies.'

'Whilst I admit finding a bag filled with ears is highly unusual, we can't jump to the conclusion that he's a murderer.'

'Course he is. One look's enough for me to tell that. I bet he drives up and down these desert highways picking up hitch-hikers just so that he can kill them and take their ears. Sick bastard!'

'Once we deal with Weizak, I'll put in a full report. Until then, I think we'll just have to keep him tied up in the back.' Thoughtfully, Dawson glanced at his companion. 'I'm beginning to think it's you.'

Stoker lit a cigarette. 'What do you mean?'

'I think you attract these crazies. I mean, what do you think the chances are of us flagging down one psycho . . . while hunting for another one?'

'I'm obviously blessed,' Stoker responded sarcastically, his face an unsmiling, grim mask of determination. 'Anyway, I bet there are hundreds of weirdoes out here. Folk disappear all the time. The fact that we've caught one is nothing but a bonus.'

Dawson turned uneasily in his seat and looked at the private investigator. Outwardly, his companion seemed relaxed, but it was impossible to guess at the turmoil which might have been raging in his brain. He too was struggling to process all they had discovered in the past few days. It seemed like an age had passed since he had been called out to investigate Hansby's death though it had only been a few days. The memory of that initial sight, which had materialised spectrally as he had walked through the mist, would be one that would stay with him for a very long time. His memory of Chartair's corpse, mangled and shredded by the tennis net, would be with him until he died.

The pick-up truck bounced and rattled along the dirt track.

Dawson was driving as fast as he dared. He could see traces of the destruction caused by the 'twister'. Stunted cacti had been torn from the earth and rocks lay cracked and splintered. The desert fauna had not escaped its fury, as evidenced by the widely scattered corpses of lizards, jackrabbits, gophers and even a coyote. Now that they were approaching the beginning of Wilder's totem markers, he could see that they too had been destroyed.

Tyres crunched over a fractured bison skull.

Suddenly, at the farthest bend of the track, less than two hundred yards away, there was a vibrant neon-blue flash — like a lightning strike — which was followed almost instantaneously by a thirty foot high shower of glowing sparks.

'Jesus!' Dawson stepped down on the brake pedal and the pick-up truck skidded to a halt.

'My money's on that being Weizak, not Jesus,' Stoker joked. 'Anyhow, it could be that the electric fence has taken care of him — fried the bastard.'

'I think we should go on foot from here. I want to see what's happening before we commit to anything.' Dawson got out. After briefly checking on their captive and ensuring that he was alive but still unconscious, he came to meet Stoker at the front of the pick-up truck.

The sound of raised voices could be heard although from this distance it was impossible to make out the words.

'You know, if this turns nasty we could have one mother of a bloodbath on our hands,' said Stoker.

'Well, there's no means of getting any back-up.' Dawson had not planned for this outcome. He had counted on Conway being more co-operative and amenable to their suggestion of taking him to somewhere safe. Weizak's presence, assuming it was him, was an unexpected turn of events — one which presented considerable dangers. His nerves were afire at the prospect of facing such an individual; someone who possessed powers almost beyond human understanding — powers which defied scientific laws and norms.

Using the cover provided by numerous boulders, Stoker and Dawson clambered to a vantage point where they could see down into the depression that housed Wilder's compound. They crept closer.

At the gate, a plume of dark smoke spiralled into the sky; however the weird miasma had largely dissipated. Wispy trails of blackness drifted away, evaporated almost, to reveal a lone, dishevelled figure.

The main gate to the compound swung open and Wilder stepped out.

10

Return of the Prodigal Son

Fascinated, Dawson stared from where he crouched alongside Stoker, looking at the pitiful wreck of a man who leant against a battered motorbike in conversation with Wilder. To all outward appearance there was nothing powerful about him at all, quite the opposite in fact. He could hear clearly enough to know that Weizak was begging for help; for forgiveness. There had been no questions asked about Conway, leading him to think that perhaps Weizak was ignorant of the fact that the psychic debunker had taken refuge here. It was equally possible that he had come here, not in search of further vengeance, but had run back to the only person who would understand, perhaps in a desire to recant his sins and return to the fold. What he could hear, supported that latter supposition.

'I didn't mean to hurt them. You've got to believe me, but I got so angry! Why didn't they just give me my money?' Weizak was almost crying. 'If they'd just done the right thing it would've been okay. Imagine what I could've done with that money. Imagine how I could've helped in — '

'Andrei, they did a bad thing, I agree, but their punishment was not justified,' Wilder interrupted.

'Those bastards started it! I showed them what I could do and *still* they cheated me! Everyone cheats me.'

'That's not true.' Wilder spoke calmly, his voice even and almost soporific. 'You have been taught how filled with deceit the world outside can be. But you have friends here. Those who love you and share your pain. Now is the time to put aside your anger, to lay down your weapons and become one of the 'Children' once more. Return unto us so that — '

'I . . . I can't. The rage . . . ' Gripping his head, Weizak fell to his knees. 'It's like a fire, burning deep inside.'

'I can take it away. There is a ritual that can release you.'

'A *ritual?* What do you mean?'

'I can take away your power; purge you of the thing that killed those men.'

Weizak stared up at Wilder, his face a contorted mask of mixed emotions. 'Take the power away?'

'Yes. Free you of its burden. You learned too much, Andrei, far too quickly.' Wilder moved nearer to the young man. 'Your thought-forms have become corrupt. Never before have I seen that vile darkness that enshrouded you and which my defences have cleansed you of . . . but it will return. Even now, I can sense it welling inside you, eager to consume you. It is fuelled by your pain.'

'I need to know. Am I responsible?'

'For the murders? Yes . . . and no.' Wilder spoke with compassion. 'Your *tulpa* ultimately destroyed them, but it was *you* who found where they lived. *You* pursued them. *You* must bear some of the blame.'

Weizak looked up, pleadingly, at Wilder. 'Is there still a place for me?'

'There may be. If I can take the power away from you,' Wilder said levelly.

'I *have* to come with you! What's it all been for otherwise?' Weizak insisted.

'Let me perform the ritual, let me take it away.' Wilder held out his hand to the young man at his feet.

'Take it away,' Weizak repeated. 'Or just take it?' A change seemed to come over him and his head tilted slightly to one side. 'You want it for yourself, don't you?'

'You are mistaken. I already have the power and have been a vessel for it for many years. We are both powder kegs, Andrei, the difference being I ensure my fuse is never lit.'

Weizak began to shake his head in distress. 'You're not going to let me come with you, are you? I've broken the tenets. But it wasn't really me! You've got to understand!'

'There may still be a way — '

'No! I remember how you looked at me before I left. You were envious, jealous because I was so much more powerful than you could ever be.' The younger man got to his feet, a mad look in his tear-filled eyes. 'All my life people have taken things from me. *You!* You're no different from those bastards I killed. Well, now you'll pay. You'll all pay! If I can't leave this stinking planet then no one will.'

The motorbike suddenly rose into the air and was then hurled by an invisible force straight at Wilder who just managed to leap clear at the last moment. His composure broken, the prophet made a mad dash for the entry gate and leapt inside as, with a resounding crash, the motorbike smashed heavily against the hastily closed gate.

Sparks flew. A sudden bright arc of electricity struck Weizak, transfixing him to the spot. His entire body shook. His unkempt hair burst into flames. He then slumped to the ground, a column of smoke rising from him.

'Well ... I guess that's it then. Case closed,' Stoker muttered.

Inside the compound, several of Wilder's followers rushed over to help their spiritual leader.

Dawson and Stoker clambered down

from the dusty ridge and walked cautiously over to the smouldering figure on the ground. Now close, they could see that Weizak's eyes were still open and that they were ablaze with a dark green, lambent light.

'Get in!' Wilder yelled from the gate. 'Hurry!' He was beckoning frantically.

Weizak got to his feet. A dark smudge of mist formed around him. It thickened, wreathing him in blackness. Dust and grit and loose bits of metal began to fly in the air as though there was a whirlwind raging all around him.

The entry gate began to buckle and bend in on itself.

Inside the compound, several rusty, empty oil drums rose off the ground and began to spiral.

Windows shattered.

Stoker fired off three shots at Weizak. The bullets never reached their target, deflected by an invisible barrier.

With a crash, the entry gate was torn from its support.

'Come on! We have to get under cover!' Fighting his way through the maelstrom of flying dust and debris, Dawson ran for the entrance, the private investigator close on his heels.

One of the *Children of Haggai* had been stationed in the lookout tower. He took aim with his AK-47, then fired a sustained burst at Weizak, the bullets disintegrating on contact with the mystical shield.

Hearing the deafening gunfire, Dawson turned in time to see three heavy car tyres take to the air. One struck the gunman full on. Screaming, the unfortunate was then dragged by an invisible force from the lookout tower and dropped on top of the barbed metal fence which immediately started to entwine around him, shredding him to the bone.

Two women in faded combat fatigues, each armed with assault rifles, ran past. One reached for a hand grenade clipped to her belt, removed the pin and then fumbled her throw.

Dawson hurled himself forward as a moment later there came a tremendous blast of shrapnel and flame. Ears ringing from the thunderous explosion, jarred and shaken by the blast, he held his arms over his head as bits of debris and body parts fell all about him. There was a tinkle of shattered glass, the licking of red-tongued flame at the edge of his vision. For a moment, he lay half-conscious, struggling to focus all of his senses. Then, choking and coughing, he painfully hoisted himself to his feet, aware that the private investigator was doing likewise.

More gunfire erupted.

Dawson and Stoker staggered after Wilder, who, accompanied by some of his followers, was heading for the entrance to the subterranean complex.

With a crash, one of the electricity pylons fell to the ground.

'We must get the book,' Wilder insisted. 'It's the only thing that might work.' He ran for the lift.

'I thought the electricity was supposed to stop him!' Dawson said as he got inside.

'It was . . . but, there was always an outside chance that it might amplify his powers,' admitted Wilder. He pulled the lever and the lift began to descend.

A deafening series of explosions shook the underground shaft.

Dawson tensed, fearing that the cables were going to snap, sending the lift into a freefall.

Reaching the bottom, Wilder flung the gate aside and sprinted for the heavy reinforced door, Dawson and Stoker only yards behind him.

Dust drizzled from the low ceiling.

There were three men, all armed, standing in front of the door to the sanctuary.

Conway peered nervously from behind them. 'For God's sake! What's happening?'

'Weizak's here!' Dawson shouted.

'Quick! Everyone inside!' Wilder ordered. He grabbed hold of Conway and rushed him down the passage to the inner chamber. Once he, Dawson, Stoker, Conway and five of his disciples were safe, he hastily closed the steel portal.

'Hurry it up for Christ's sake!' Conway shouted desperately. 'Use that spell!'

Wilder began leafing through the pages of the *Bardo Thodol*. 'Here it is. Please don't interrupt me once I've started.'

'But, how's this going to work?'

Dawson was confused. He looked at the metal door as though half-expecting it to burst open. 'Don't you have to be in the same room with Weizak or something?'

Wilder shook his head. 'No. As long as he hears my words that should suffice.'

'This place is like a goddamn vault!' Dawson exclaimed. 'How's he going to hear you?'

'Calm yourself,' Wilder replied. He strode to the desk he habitually preached from, opened a drawer and took out a microphone. 'I had this installed so that my voice can be heard by all. Now, be quiet.' Clearly and concisely, he started to read.

Having never had the need or the desire to study Ancient Tibetan, Dawson could not understand any of the words that poured from the prophet's lips. Down here, he could only imagine what might be happening on the surface. What he had seen that day had far exceeded anything he had ever experienced before and, despite his training, he was struggling to come to terms with it.

The incantation went on, Wilder's voice

maintaining a hypnotic monotone; each word perfectly pronounced and eloquently enunciated as they were transmitted through an array of strategically concealed and positioned loudspeakers. For the best part of three minutes he droned on.

And then . . . silence; a deathly hush.

'Do you . . . do you think it's worked?' asked Conway, wild-eyed.

'I suppose the only way to find out would be to open the door,' Wilder replied tentatively.

'No way!' Conway exclaimed.

'I, for one, am not going to stay — ' Stoker was cut off by an almighty crack on the door.

'Oh Jesus,' Conway whimpered fearfully.

The door began to edge open; the steel bolts warping under incredible pressure. Then, with a resounding clang that reverberated throughout the chamber, it flew wide.

Weizak stood on the threshold, his eyes ablaze, that dark aura surrounding his scrawny and blackened frame. His eyes widened with recognition on seeing

Conway who stood next to Wilder. 'I should've known you'd be here.' Menacingly, he advanced into the room.

'It hasn't worked!' Conway shrieked, his words bordering on the pathetic. 'That damned spell's done nothing!'

'Don't hurt him, Andrei. He's an innocent. He recognised the truth of the *tulpa*,' Wilder urged.

'An innocent? There *are* no innocents,' Weizak shrieked. Like an ethereal pseudopod, the black miasma snaked out from him and struck the nearest of the prophet's children. Screaming, the man was hurled against the far wall of the chamber.

Suddenly, the sanctuary rang with ear-splitting gunshots as Stoker and the remaining cultists opened fire, releasing a massive hail of bullets.

Once again, Weizak was unharmed. 'Can't you see, that does nothing!' he sneered. A second wraith-like appendage made a grab for Dawson who threw himself to one side, narrowly dodging the attack.

'Over here!' Wilder shouted.

Dawson spun round and saw that

Wilder was beckoning to him. In the next instant, the image of a glowing man — like a shadow in reverse — stepped out of the prophet.

The spectral figure spread its arms, creating a barrier; bathing Wilder and Conway in a golden effulgence from which Weizak's darkness recoiled.

Dawson, Stoker and the remaining four *Children of Haggai* ran for the safety of Wilder's astral projection. The slowest of them — a shaven-headed black woman with a weird purple tattoo on her forehead — fell to the floor, clutching her throat as the dark mist wreathed itself about her, constricting her like a python. Rapaciously, a tenebrous tendril fastened around one of her legs and lifted her off the floor. It then started to swing her back and forth like a pendulum before throwing her aside.

'How do we stop the bastard?' Stoker yelled at Wilder. 'Can that . . . thing of yours fight him?'

Wilder was too concentrated on his *tulpa* — his mystical twin, his own thought-form — to answer. Eyes closed, he began to mouth strange sounds. The glow around his incorporeal double began to intensify, providing much needed illumination to the chamber. Glints of gleaming purple, crimson and blue light shone within the otherworldly aura.

Weizak retreated. His features were indistinct, half-visible through the black, suffocating shadows that billowed out around him. Then, in an awesome clash of power, his negative energies lunged forward and began engulfing the golden form; rending it, stretching it like rubber in an attempt to tear it asunder.

Dawson could hardly believe what he was seeing. For a fleeting moment, his rational mind tried to dismiss the psychic confrontation that was playing out before his eyes. Then some kind of lucidity returned and, realising that Wilder was on the verge of collapse with the strain he was being forced to exert, he hastily scanned the chamber for an alternative escape route, knowing full well that this was a battle neither he nor Stoker could win.

With a blinding flash, Wilder's *tulpa* vanished.

Then something completely unexpected happened.

Weizak stumbled, an arm outstretched to support himself. He reeled drunkenly; a confused look on his face. Then the amorphous entity which emanated from him began to condense as it was drawn back into his body. Coughing violently, he fell to his knees, his *tulpa* now pouring into his mouth and nostrils — intoxicating the core of his being with a deluge of negative and destructive emotions. Writhing in agony, he kicked out violently; dark, oleaginous foam flying from his lips. His fingers were clenched tight and the veins and arteries of his neck were prominently corded. His eyes had become black, doll-like; wide and staring as though they had seen something which transcended the human concept of horror.

'The ... the spell! It's working!' Conway shouted ecstatically.

To Dawson's mind, what he was witnessing was a sort of anti-exorcism, one in which the unwanted, malign force was not being expelled from its host but rather driven back inside.

Weizak was shaking as though in the throes of an extreme epileptic shock, his body continuing to vacuum up the rapidly thinning black smoke. Soon there was no more and, with a final, violent jolt, he lost consciousness, unable to endure the wracking pain any longer.

'He's dying,' Conway shouted.

'He's dead.' Stoker stepped forward, pointed his .45 at Weizak and was just about to pull the trigger when Dawson knocked his arm aside.

'He's wanted alive, remember?' Dawson looked to Wilder who stood, breathing heavily, his strangely saurian features etched with fatigue. 'Is this what that spell was supposed to do?'

Wearily, Wilder nodded.

'What's the good of that?' Stoker demanded.

'Think of it as returning the genie to the bottle,' Wilder answered. He wavered uncertainly for a moment until one of his disciples helped in supporting him. 'Now, all we have to do is ensure that his emotions are constantly kept in check. I am in possession of a certain drug which — ' He stopped abruptly on seeing Weizak spring to his feet.

Gone was the inky darkness which had consumed him and which *he* had now consumed. Staring uncertainly at the armed men stood before him, Weizak then turned and fled.

'Don't let him escape!' Dawson shouted, taking up the chase. Past the now ruined vault door and across the hallway he ran, Stoker close behind. His pulse was racing, his heart hammering in his chest, thudding against his ribs as he sped down the underground passage. And then he heard the lift gate being closed, followed a moment later by the noisy grating of its ascent. A faint inrush of warm, dusty wind sighed along the tunnel and touched his face, heating the sweat which lay in a cold film on his forehead.

'*Shit!*' Stoker cursed. Futilely, he thumped the 'call' button.

'I guess we'll have to wait for it to come down.' The best part of a minute elapsed before Dawson heard the faint clang from above which signalled the arrival of the

lift to the outside world and Weizak's
probable escape.

★   ★   ★

Dusk was beginning to fall, creating a
serene wash of indigo across the sky. The
first stars were visible and the light from
the rising moon bathed the desert
landscape in a soft glow.

'Wonder what Weizak will do when he
discovers his 'passenger',' Dawson commented as, from the wrecked gate of the
compound, he watched the old pick-up
truck fade into the darkening distance
and then vanish from sight. Silently, he
cursed himself for not having taken the
keys with him when he had left but he
consoled himself with the belief that Weizak
would undoubtedly have been more than
capable of hot-wiring the vehicle.

'Christ knows. Maybe, in a few years'
time, some road construction engineer
will find his earless corpse. That's if the
coyotes don't get to him first.' Stoker
struck a match, lit a cigarette and took a
drag. He cast a disapproving eye over the

heaped mounds of junk, vehicle parts and scavenged miscellanea. 'You'd have thought, with all this crap lying around, that there would have been something we could have gone after him in. Shame Weizak's motor-bike's bust and Conway's car got wrecked when that pylon came down.' He kicked at the dust in an act of frustration.

Dawson turned his gaze on Conway, who sat on a chair, drinking from a bottle of *Coca-Cola*, a forlorn, exhausted look in his eyes. Nearby, Wilder could be seen giving instructions to the surviving dozen or so members of his cult. As well as the six who had been killed, nine were seriously injured.

'And guess what? There's no telephone here either,' said Stoker bitterly.

'Why doesn't that surprise me?'

Wilder walked over to join them. 'We've taken a heavy toll this day. Yet this day is not the End Day and for that we must remain eternally grateful.'

'Do you think he'll come back?' Stoker asked.

'I hope he does. I can't help him otherwise. Rest assured, he's no threat for the moment. The force which he possesses will take days, perhaps weeks to replenish and it could be that he will never be able to access it again anyway. Time will tell.' Wilder smiled tiredly.

'So, what do we do now?' Stoker scratched at his stubbled chin.

Dawson looked up. 'Well, it's not a bad night for a walk.'

'You've got to be kidding me!' Stoker exclaimed. 'It's at least eight miles to the highway, probably more.'

'We need to get word to McMasters about all of this. I can't think of a better idea, can you?' Dawson asked.

Stoker turned to Wilder. 'Are you sure there are no working vehicles left?'

'Alas, no. The remaining jeep was broken up a few days ago for the component parts,' Wilder responded. 'We have a delivery of supplies once a week but apart from that we try to avoid contact with others. We take pride in being self-sufficient. Ask not for what you do not need.'

'Damned survivalists.' Stoker threw his cigarette down and expressively ground it into the rough earth with his shoe. He thrust his hands into his pockets, hunched his shoulders and, without another word, began the long walk.

Dawson took one last look at the compound then set off after his companion.

Epilogue

Dawson's footsteps echoed strangely in the featureless corridor, lit by cold, actinic light. FBI Director Dennis Foster walked along beside him.

'We're pretty sure it must be Weizak we've got here, based on his confession, but I want someone we trust to make a positive identification,' Foster said.

'So, he just handed himself in?'

'Yes, the day before yesterday. As I'm sure you know, our efforts to find him were unsuccessful. Once we got your call, we had people out there within the hour scouring the desert but all we found was Jacob Tarrant wrapped up and dumped on the side of the road like a burrito and Wilder's kooky set-up. You probably didn't see all the stuff he had down there but he must have spent a small fortune on weapons, dry goods and drugs. The strangest thing has to be the 'spaceship' that you referred to in your report. It might have looked impressive but trust me, it's not something we need to get NASA involved with. I've seen tins of beans with more lifting capacity! Not only that, it was built in an underground cave, with no means of extraction. So the question is, how on earth were they expecting to launch it?' Foster chuckled briefly.

'Presumably Wilder had some kind of mystical explanation,' Dawson suggested. 'Could be it was never designed to go to outer space but . . . somewhere else. A different dimension or some such.'

'I'd believe anything of that bunch. Anyhow, all of them are currently housed here, pending further investigation into possible criminal activity. We can definitely get Wilder — fraud, use of controlled substances, that kind of thing. Unfortunately, most of the others have been indoctrinated to the point where you can't have a meaningful conversation with them. They remain convinced that the end of the world is imminent and only Wilder can lead them to salvation. Strange thing is, it's not a fear of being nuked by the Soviets or some devastating epidemic that has them all so worried but rather the return of some being from outer space known as the 'Old One'. Christ knows who or what that's meant to be.'

'What about Randall Conway?'

'He's going to be fine, physically at least. He was pretty resistant to being sworn to secrecy on all of this. I gather he's lost the discovery of a lifetime. Still, he's agreed to join our team of researchers. I daresay he'll prove useful.' Passing several white-coated technicians, Foster took Dawson to a small surveillance chamber with one large, darkened window.

Beyond the two-way mirror, was a cell-like room with one occupant.

Dawson nodded slowly. 'That's him.'

Weizak was sitting calmly at a table with a black briefcase on it from which he was telekinetically removing banknotes and piling them in high, precariously balanced stacks.

Dawson took a deep breath, fighting back a pang of fear. Only the thickness of a glass screen separated him from a man he was only too aware could kill with the power of his mind alone.

'Good,' said Foster. 'Now that he's calmed down, he appears to be quite content to stay here. He's been counting that hundred thousand we gave him — over and over, and he's been reasonably cooperative; allowing us to run a few tests on him.'

'I see that his powers have obviously returned.'

'Yes. It was simply a case of getting him to re-focus his emotions. Your suggestion about the prize money does seem to have worked. All this guy wanted was to get what was owed to him. I dare say in time he'll want to leave and we might have an issue with that but we're working on some techniques that will hopefully enable us to harness his ability. I think so long as we don't piss him off we should be safe. Wilder has also been able to persuade him that he can still go with the others in the 'spaceship' when the 'stars are right' and this 'Old One' decides to put in an appearance. Its complete bullshit, of course, but it helps to keep him in line.'

Dawson regarded the solitary figure for

a moment in silence, then he turned to Foster. 'So, what's the verdict on the *Bardo Thodol*? On *all* of this?'

'Now that was interesting. We've got top men looking at it right now. Conway told us that he was bequeathed it by an elderly colleague who acquired it under mysterious circumstances. From what we've pieced together, on his travels, Wilder had discovered how to unlock this power but had never been motivated to use it in a particularly dramatic way. Weizak, on the other hand, was getting out of control even when he was part of the cult. In fact, Wilder was considering expelling him before he left of his own accord. Seems that Weizak had aspirations of returning in triumph, having scooped the prize money from *Chartair's Challenge*. His motivation was probably to get back into Wilder's good books and to help finance work on the 'spaceship'. As for the *Bardo Thodol* itself — well, that happens to be rather unique.'

'Unique? What do you mean?'

'I mean that only Tuska Grembi's version of the text has the instructions about

255

how to negate a malevolent *tulpa*. You'd probably be dead now if it weren't for that.'

'Christ,' Dawson said wearily. 'If Hamilton had just paid up, all of this could have been avoided.'

Foster nodded. 'True. But some good may come of it. Looking at the bigger picture, we now have access to a potentially game-changing asset for our country. Just stop for a moment and think of the potential.'

'It's exactly that which worries me,' Dawson admitted. He had talked about his concerns with Stoker on their long walk from Wilder's compound a week ago. The hard-boiled private investigator had asserted his view that the kind of power Weizak had wielded was too volatile and depended too much on the capricious nature of the individual. Stoker had been vocal in expressing his opinion that the world would be better off without it. By the time they had hitched a lift and got to the nearest phone, Dawson felt the same way.

'Just be glad that it's us who have this asset, not one of our enemies,' Foster said, brusquely. 'You did well. You and Mr Stoker. We've arranged for all the charges against him to be dropped by the way.'

'That's good. He deserves a break.'

'Well, on what we paid for his services he could take a very long vacation. Probably best if he does just that.'

Dawson's eyes kept slipping back to the darkened window and the solitary figure beyond it. 'Sir, are you sure you can contain Weizak here?'

'Without doubt,' Foster said. He opened the door and led Dawson out. 'He's our concern now. Your involvement has been much appreciated and there'll probably be a promotion in this for you, but you should just forget about this case. You've read the official line, I hope?'

'Yes, sir. The murders, along with several others, were committed by one Jacob Tarrant, long-term resident of Barstow and psychopath. He protests his innocence of course but ample evidence was found to prove his guilt. The unusual means of death are to be suppressed and anyone who can remember otherwise, paid off.'

'You've got it!' Foster patted Dawson on the shoulder as they walked back to the exit. 'That was a stroke of luck, you two finding that sick son of a bitch. Keeps things nice and neat.' He stopped in front of the door that led out of the secure area. 'You should take a vacation too. Get away from it all for a while. I'll square it with McMasters.'

'Thank you, sir. I might just do that.' Dawson turned and left. He could see which way the wind was blowing. Any fears he had about the wisdom of studying Weizak would not be tolerated. The case would not be talked about again, at least not the true case, and if he toed the line, his success in the Bureau was assured. An image of the mangled corpse of Max Chartair seemed to hang in his memory. The news agencies had finally been allowed to report on the television presenter's death and his face had been all over the papers along with sanitised details of the murder. Maybe a vacation would help. Perhaps it would get the images to fade. A different picture formed in his mind. A memory of a seedy bar in Los Angeles called *The Black Oyster Bar*. He began to smile, remembering his last telephone call from Stoker. The private investigator had placed a call from Samantha De'Carlo's house. Apparently, with Wolf recuperating, the actress had persuaded Stoker to move in for a time 'to provide extra security'.

'You should come and see us,' Stoker had offered, sounding more relaxed than Dawson had known in years. 'Samantha says you're always welcome and Wolf wants to thank you for keeping him alive until the ambulance arrived. We can get drunk and not talk about any of that shit they swore me not to mention. Might even see about getting you to join the Church.'

His mind made up, Dawson left the FBI research station and climbed into his car. To hell with Bureau secrets and freakish Tibetan magic, he thought. There was a drink with his name on it in Los Angeles.

We do hope that you have enjoyed reading this large print book.

Did you know that all of our titles are available for purchase?

We publish a wide range of high quality large print books including:
Romances, Mysteries, Classics
General Fiction
Non Fiction and Westerns

Special interest titles available in large print are:
The Little Oxford Dictionary
Music Book, Song Book
Hymn Book, Service Book

Also available from us courtesy of Oxford University Press:
Young Readers' Dictionary
(large print edition)
Young Readers' Thesaurus
(large print edition)

For further information or a free brochure, please contact us at:
Ulverscroft Large Print Books Ltd.,
The Green, Bradgate Road, Anstey,
Leicester, LE7 7FU, England.
Tel: (00 44) **0116 236 4325**
Fax: (00 44) **0116 234 0205**

Other titles in the
Linford Mystery Library:

UNDERCURRENT OF EVIL

Norman Firth

After Sheila Nesbitt's father is found dead in the Thames following a visit to the Satyr Club, the most exclusive gambling parlour in town, she's determined to uncover the truth of what happened. Enlisting the help of her friend, Richard Denning, they set out to investigate what grim secrets the Satyr Club is hiding behind the suave smile of the manager, Collwell, and his sultry, seductive assistant, Lady Mercia Standard, who sets her sights on Richard. Their pursuit eventually leads them to the club's mysterious owner — 'The Old Devil'.

THE MISSING MAN

V. J. Banis

Writer Cindy Carter accepts a routine assignment from her editor: fly to Athens, write some articles, and fit in an interview with an elderly professor who insists he's got something important to say. But what occurs is anything but routine. Her case is accidentally switched with that of another passenger containing one hundred thousand dollars in cash. When the professor is killed in an explosion, Cindy becomes embroiled in an assassination plot involving a Russian terrorist, and must assist NATO agents in capturing the missing man.

BETTY BLAKE

N. M. Scott

Featuring an amazingly perceptive Edwardian child blessed with a talent for solving village puzzles, Betty Blake provides us with a glimpse of a future amateur detective in the making. Betty begins her sleuthing at age nine continuing through to age twelve. Her cases include pillar box puzzles to headless ducks, a stolen emerald ring and the death of a solicitor's wife — not to mention a ghostly disturbance on a golf course. For someone so young and precocious — no case is a burden or unsolvable!

THE TREASURE HUNTERS

Norman Firth

Gilda Baxter decides to call unannounced at her fiancé's cottage on a surprise visit . . . only to learn on her arrival that his boat, badly damaged, had been found floating overturned in the bay, and that he is missing — presumed drowned . . . Diana Russell is on a mission to help her twin sister stop a man from blackmailing and ruining her life. For her plan to succeed, she must put herself in great danger — but sometimes best laid plans have a habit of going awry . . .

SHERLOCK HOLMES: THE FOUR-HANDED GAME

Paul D. Gilbert

Holmes and Watson find themselves bombarded with an avalanche of dramatic cases! Holmes enrols Inspectors Lestrade and Bradstreet to help him play a dangerous four-handed game against an organization whose power and influence seems to know no bounds. As dissimilar as the cases seem to be — robbery, assault, and gruesome murder — Holmes suspects that each one has been meticulously designed to lure him towards a conclusion that even he could not have anticipated. However, when his brother Mycroft goes missing, he realizes that he is running out of time . . .

THE MANUSCRIPT KILLER

Noel Lee

When Detective Inspector Drizzle receives a mysterious message from elderly recluse Matthew Trevelyn imploring him to visit the next day, as he is in fear of his life, Drizzle sets out straight away. Delayed by a punctured tyre, however, he arrives at the country house to discover he's too late: Trevelyn has been brutally murdered — strangled by a silk scarf belonging to his niece. Her boyfriend had been thrown out the previous night after a raging quarrel with Trevelyn — but is he the true culprit? Thus begins Drizzle's strangest case . . .